THE
LEDBERG RUNESTONE

THE JONAH HEYWOOD CHRONICLES
- BOOK ONE -

PATRICK DONOVAN

DIVERSIONBOOKS

Also by Patrick Donovan
Demon Jack

Diversion Books
A Division of Diversion Publishing Corp.
443 Park Avenue South, Suite 1008
New York, New York 10016
www.DiversionBooks.com

This is a work of fiction. Names, characters, places and incidents either
are the product of the author's imagination or are used fictitiously.
Any resemblance to actual persons, living or dead, events or locales is
entirely coincidental.

For more information, email info@diversionbooks.com

First Diversion Books edition January 2018.
Paperback ISBN: 978-1-63576-178-8
eBook ISBN: 978-1-63576-177-1

LSIDB/1712

To Erin, for always believing in me,
even when I didn't...Jerk.

To my Pop, who was always a much better storyteller than
I'll ever be. Hopefully, I managed to pick up a few tricks.
Rest easy, Old Man.

And for G, as is everything that I do
that is even remotely worthwhile.

CHAPTER 1

"Jonah Heywood?" the woman asked, watching me from across the table.

I tore my attention from my drink and looked up at her. I was still hungover from the night before, and the coffee and booze concoction that I was currently using to chase away the pounding headache had, until a second ago, held me mostly enraptured.

"Do I know you?" I asked, stupid question though it was. I knew most of the locals that came to Jack of the Wood. I mean, I'd spent the better part of most every day of the past two years in here, ensuring that the beer taps stayed in good working order and the brew was up to snuff. Of all the bars in Asheville, it was probably my favorite. The food was good, they opened early, or early by my standards, and they served coffee. Coffee with booze. All in all, I considered it a winning combination. Winning enough, at least, that I was on my fourth Nutty Irishman, and it wasn't yet two in the afternoon.

"I don't believe so, no," she said, her voice hinting at the slightest bit of an accent. It sounded German, maybe Russian. Truth be told, I was never very good with pegging stuff like that down.

"I didn't think so. What do you want?"

"I was wondering if I could have a moment of your time?"

I finished off the last of my drink.

"For what, exactly?" I asked.

"A job offer."

I looked the woman over. She was pretty in a 1950s pin-up sort of way and curvy enough to put most modern-day girls to shame. She was tall, almost as tall as my own six feet and change. She wore her hair, a pale blonde that was bordering on white, tied back in an intricate braid that hung to her waist.

"What kind of job?" I asked.

"A lucrative one," she said.

From time to time, in my line of work, this sort of thing happens. A stranger approaches you in a public place with an offer of a job, usually touting a large sum of money and a request that tends to be, at best, legally questionable. It's not the norm, but it's not unheard of, either. Every now and again, said deals were legit. However, even when your stranger turned out to be on the up and up working for, or with, someone you didn't know, was risky.

I stared at her, trying to weigh my options. On the one hand, I didn't know this woman from Adam. On the other, I needed the money. Not just needed the money, I was hurting for it. I decided to hear her out. Nothing said I had to accept her little job offer if I didn't like what I heard.

"I'll tell you what. You wanna buy me another round, I suppose we could chat for a few."

She stared at me for a moment, one brow quirked, then finally nodded and went to the bar. I watched her go, trying to remember if I had seen her somewhere and was just getting too drunk to remember. She came back a moment later, setting another drink on the table. I used my cane to push out the chair opposite of the one I was sitting in, primarily to keep the table between us. She sat down, all casual grace and confidence, and slid the drink over to me. I wrapped my hands around it, letting the warmth from the coffee radiate through the cup and into the palms of my hand.

"So," I said, taking another sip. "It's your dime."

"Then I'll get straight to the point. I've heard stories about you, Mister Heywood, that you possess a certain way about you. It just so happens that I'm in need of a man with your particular skillset."

I quirked a brow.

"And what, pray tell, have you heard?" I asked.

"It's my understanding that you're something of an expert on the occult, at least in comparison to the local population. I also understand you're quite the accomplished liar and thief. You possess more than a few, shall we say, less common talents," she said, meeting my gaze without so much as a twitch.

I put my cup on the table and ran a hand through my hair. She was right, of course. I was the only spell-slinging, dream-walking, spirit-talking, magic-making shaman around these parts. At least, I was the only one that I knew of. She was also right in saying that I had a bit of a reputation amongst the locals. Especially among those who were involved in the more spooky side of things. Whether that reputation was for good or ill was mostly dependent on who you asked.

"Is that assessment far from the truth?" she asked.

"For the sake of conversation, let's assume that it's not," I said. "How about you tell me what this job is all about."

"It was an item that belonged to my husband. Aside from being quite valuable, it possesses more than a little bit of sentimental value. It was stolen recently, and it's come to my attention that it is now somewhere within your fine city."

"So call the police."

"I'm afraid that isn't an option."

"Alright. Let's assume for a moment that I am interested in tracking this down, what exactly is it that I would be acquiring?" I asked.

"Are you familiar with Ledberg Runestone?" she asked.

"I think I saw a documentary on it once, but I wouldn't say I'm familiar. Refresh my memory."

She nodded.

"Runestones are national treasures in Scandinavia. They depict art and stories ranging back to the time of the Vikings. The Ledberg stone, according to some, is a depiction of a very famous story of Norse mythology. My husband acquired a piece of this artifact. Much like many of the things my husband was involved in, he used less than reputable sources in acquiring it."

"Which explains why you can't call the police."

"Precisely," she said.

I settled back in my chair and stared at her over the rim

of my cup. My hangover was mostly gone now, the ache in my head reduced to a distant, minor discomfort. She'd picked the right time to ask, I'll give her that. Conning desperate folks with fake exorcisms wasn't exactly a booming business. It paid the bills, I suppose, but I'd been doing it so long that I had to travel to Boone, Hickory, and in some cases, all the way out to Greensboro to find work where people didn't know my name or my face. On rare occasions I did chase away an actual spirit, so it wasn't all dishonest work.

Only most of the time.

I gave the woman another once-over. She wasn't wearing much in the way of jewelry. A simple pendant at the hollow of her throat hung on a leather cord. She wore a cuff-style bracelet that looked like it was silver, but could have just as easily have been made of pewter. Her clothes—a light jacket, jeans, and a black button-up shirt that clung to her figure—didn't exactly scream massive bank account. Sure, she could have been one of the folks that didn't want to flaunt their money, but in my experience those people were a rarity.

"Let's suppose, for the sake of conversation, that I were to take your job. What kind of pay are we talking about?"

"Ten thousand dollars up front, and another ten thousand when I have possession of the stone."

Twenty grand. That was a lot of money. Enough for me to pay off a few debts and take some time off. A few months would be enough time to let things settle down and for my name to get out of circulation, at least locally.

It was tempting. Hell, it was more than tempting. Which is exactly why I had to turn her down.

I've been in this game for a while and, like in most things, when an offer came along that seemed too good to be true, it usually was. In less than legal lines of work, it could mean anything from a run-in with the cops to a potentially fatal set up from the competition.

"I think I'm going to have to pass," I finally said. "Thanks for the drink."

"Can I ask why?"

I emptied my cup and set it on the table.

"Honestly?"

She nodded.

"Two reasons. First, you're offering me twenty thousand dollars to go steal some rock. Sentimental value or not, that's a lot of money. Second, I've never met you. I have no idea who you are."

"I can assure you, I'm not a police officer if that's your concern."

"Right, anyhow. I'm not sure what movies you've seen, but you can hire folks to do ludicrously stupid things for a lot less than twenty grand."

"I'm not interested in hiring someone else. I'm interested in hiring you."

"And I'm not buying what you're selling," I said. "Which means your shit out of luck. Sorry lady."

"I see. Is there anything I can offer you that would make you reconsider?"

"Afraid not," I said.

The noonday sun shining in through the windows and reflecting off the bar gave the woman's skin a warm, radiant glow. I was well on my way towards being good and drunk by now. A small, less civilized part of my brain argued that maybe there was something she could do, something that involved a much different setting and far fewer clothes. Granted, the sober, rational part of my brain was also chiming in to let me know that I was being an asshole. I opted to make that part of my brain the part that I listened to.

"I see. I'm sorry to hear that," she said.

"Yeah, well, that's how these things go sometimes."

She stood, reached into her jacket and set a twenty on the table, sliding it towards me. A plain, white business card was folded into the bill.

"What's this?" I asked, picking up twenty and the card.

"The money is for your lunch. Eat something. I think it would be in your best interest to try and sober up before you leave."

I gave the card a once-over. A telephone number with an area code I didn't recognize had been written on one side.

"This is my calling card, for when you decide to change your mind," she said.

"Don't hold your breath," I said.

She stared at me for another second, then turned, weaving her way through the growing crowd. I took about half of her advice. I spent the next hour putting down a plate of fish and chips, along with a few Green Man IPAs. It didn't do much in the way of sobering me up, but the food did help to clear my head just a little bit.

When I finally mustered up the energy to head home, it was pushing sunset. The cane and the ache in my left leg were a constant reminder of the last time I'd tried to do the right thing.

I said my goodbyes to the regulars and the bartender on my way to the door and stepped out into the early

November chill. In the distance, the sun was sinking behind the horizon, highlighting the sky in a myriad of reds and purples. Moments like these left me awestruck by just how much I love this damned city.

I'd parked my truck, a Chevy Short Bed from the mid-seventies, less than a block away, in a small lot that sits between the little strip of buildings housing Jack's and a store that sold futons. A few years back, this truck had been a rusted-out heap of junk. My father and I rebuilt it from the ground up, turning a broken husk of American metal into an object of pure sex and steel wrapped up in flat black and chrome.

I'd almost made it to my truck when a Cadillac pulled in. It was an older model, not quite old enough to be considered a classic, but old enough to have lost a lot of what made it a luxury car. The driver came so close to hitting me that, if it hadn't been for my cane, I'd have probably taken a face full of pavement trying to get out of the way. Instead, I merely stumbled into some poor bastard's Honda hard enough to leave a Jonah-sized dent in his hood. The driver parked the Caddy sideways, blocking the rest of the lot off from the street.

The Cadillac sat there idling for a moment before all four doors opened and the occupants piled out. I didn't recognize the driver or the guy that came out of the passenger side, but the two that got out of the backseat, Waylon Carver and his brother Cash—those two I knew.

I also knew that my night had just taken a very, very painful turn.

CHAPTER 2

"Well, well, well. Imagine my surprise, finding Jonah Heywood stumbling out of a bar," Waylon said. Of the two Carver Brothers, he was the biggest. He was easily six and a half feet tall and built like a professional strongman. I'm not talking bodybuilder big either. He looked more like a contestant from the shows where big scary guys flip over tractor tires, carry boulders, and pull trucks. He could break me in half with about as much effort as it would take me to crush a beer can.

Cash, on the other hand, was short, wiry, with corded, ropy muscle and about nine different kinds of crazy. They both shared the same dark hair and dark eyes, though Waylon wore his in a ponytail while his brother just looked like he needed a haircut. Both wore jeans, button-up shirts and cowboy boots, and neither one of them was a fan of yours truly. They were also the closest thing that these parts had to organized crime, a throwback to the fabled Dixie Mafia that used to run rampant in the South during the seventies and eighties. Logic dictated that the other two with them were the hired help. Logic also dictated that there was a damned good chance that any passerby who saw anything would, in the in the interest of not wanting to end up in traction, just keep on passing by. It was the better part of common sense to keep one's mouth shut rather than risk the Carver brothers taking note of some do-gooder's good deed.

"Waylon, Cash. How's it going fellas?" I said, trying my best to keep the tremor of fear out of my voice.

"Well, you know how it is Jonah. Tough times and all," Waylon said, shoving his hands into the front pockets of his jeans.

Cash, on the other hand, was perfectly content to watch me with the stare of a hungry lion watching a gazelle.

The other two men were flanking me now. That left Waylon and Cash in front of me, and a stone wall behind me.

"How about you, Cash, how you doing?" Waylon asked.

"Not so good, Waylon. Money's kind of tight right now," Cash said, his voice a dull, unwavering monotone.

"What about you two? Stevie, Ray, how you boys doing?" Waylon asked, his voice still full of mocking good cheer.

"Struggle is real, brother," Stevie nodded.

"Man, I hate to hear that," I said, trying to keep my eyes on all four at the same time.

"Well, it's funny you should mention that."

"Oh?"

"Yes sir," Waylon said. "Considering you owe us—how much is it, Cash?"

"The initial loan was ten thousand dollars. I haven't calculated the interest."

"Right, the several thousand dollars you owe us. Pay us that and me and my brother, my boys here? Why, we'll be in the land of milk and honey."

"Yeah, about that," I said.

"Don't do it, Jonah. Don't tell me what I think it is you're about to tell me," Waylon said.

"I don't think he has our money, Waylon," Cash chimed in.

"Jonah, is that true? You don't have it?" Waylon asked, mock disappointment creeping into his tone.

"Not right now," I said, "but I can get it."

Waylon shook his head, letting out a long, slow sigh. Stevie and Ray had both managed to move in closer while my attention had been on Waylon and Cash. By now, desperation and fear had succeeded in chasing away most of the drunken cloud I'd spent the last several hours building around myself. Now the reality of my situation was really starting to sink in with a startling clarity. I'd borrowed a sizable chunk of money from some really, really bad people. I'd thought I'd be able to pull off something to get it all paid up quick, and surely before it came down to this. I'd been wrong. Now, I was two seconds from getting my skull caved in.

"Jonah. Jonah, Jonah, Jonah, why, man? Why would you put me in this position? I mean, how long have we been friends? What? Five years now?" Waylon said.

I opened my mouth to say something, but Stevie, or

maybe it was Ray, I wasn't sure yet, kicked my cane out from underneath me. My bad leg buckled and I fell to the ground in a rather ungraceful heap, which hurt my pride more than anything. When I tried to stand, the other guy I'd yet to match with a name planted a cowboy boot right into my gut. This one hurt, knocking the breath out of me and turning the booze in my stomach into a hot, churning mass. It took everything I had to keep from throwing up all over the little silver caps on the tips of Waylon's pointy boots.

Waylon crouched in front of me, resting his elbows on his knees. The smell of sweat and pot smoke rolled off of him in waves, and I had to double the fight to keep the stuff inside my stomach from relocating to the outside of my stomach. Waylon reached out and grabbed a handful of my hair, tilting my head back far enough that I could see up into his face.

"Jonah, you need to understand something. We're pals and all, but you've screwed with my money. That's how I feed my kids." He let go of my hair and stood. Stevie and Ray both grabbed an arm and hauled me up to my knees, wrenching my bad leg in a way that was about as far from pleasant as humanly possible. Waylon had my cane in one hand, slapping it against his palm in a slow, threatening rhythm.

"A lot of money, Jonah," Waylon explained. "That's what you owe me."

"I'm aware," I said.

"Oh? You're aware? Well shit, Jonah," Waylon said, his voice loud, mocking. "You're aware that you owe me a lot of money, and I'm assuming that you're aware that every week you don't pay, the interest gets tacked onto the principal."

Waylon turned to stare at me, his eyes going cold.

"I'm sure you're also aware," he said, punctuating his point with an open-handed slap to the side of my head, "that you are in a fucking world of hurt right now."

Waylon nodded and in unison both Stevie and Ray threw me backwards, hard, into the stone wall that bordered the parking lot. My head bounced against it, and everything got distant and far away, the ringing in my ears picking up what felt like a few hundred extra decibels. I wasn't exactly sure who it was that hit me next, but whoever it was landed a shot that left my mouth filled with the taste of my own blood.

I went down and the next few minutes consisted of a lot of pain. I tried to do the best I could to protect my head and ribs, but I was pretty sure one of them even landed a few shots on me with my cane. When it finally ended, I was bleeding from a cut on my lip and both nostrils. My sides, my stomach, and my arms all felt like one massive bruise, but as far as I could tell, I was mostly intact. I hurt like hell, but I was intact.

"Get him up," Waylon said.

Stevie and Ray pulled me up onto my knees for a second time. Waylon stood in front of me, casually leaning on my cane.

"So, Jonah, here's the situation. I'm guessing a busy guy like you, what with the ripping folks off and making a very valiant attempt at drinking your liver into a coma, just forgot about me. Which, while it hurts my feelings, happens. I get that. So, to make sure it doesn't happen again, Cash's going to leave you with a reminder about the importance of remembering who your friends are," Waylon said, explaining this to me in the same tone of voice one uses with a difficult child. "See, this way, we don't have to worry about another tragic misunderstanding. That's what I'm chalking this up to, by the way, a big misunderstanding. I don't want to believe that you'd just forget all about me like that, what with us being friends and all."

My right eye had swollen shut, so I couldn't see Cash. I did, however, hear the demented little freak all but panting in anticipation, which made me more than just a little nervous. I struggled, trying to break away from the toughs that were holding me. I succeeded in provoking Waylon into slapping me again, and for a moment the world threatened to go dark. I was fighting to hang onto consciousness as it was, but at this point I wasn't sure if it would make much of a difference. I heard the clicking of a box cutter's blade sliding out of its handle a second before Cash pressed it just below my temple. A line of warmth slid its way down the side of my face, following the blade as he pulled it down over my cheek, all the way to my jawline. I could feel blood, hot against the chill air, coursing down my face and over my neck.

"Now Jonah, because I'm a nice guy, I'm going to give you twenty-four hours to pay me something. At least the interest, can you do that for me?" Waylon said.

I nodded.

"I'm sorry, I couldn't hear that."

"Yeah," I choked out, "Yeah, I can do that."

"I hope so," Waylon said reaching into his pocket and withdrawing a photograph. He held it up in front of my eyes. It was a shot of my father walking from his car to his front door, taken from a distance. He was wearing his work clothes. I could see the engine grease that stained the front of his jeans. He had a bad habit of wiping his hands on his pants while he was working. "See, we have this policy that if the Lendee can't pay the Lender, then we have to collect from their next available kin. In this case, well, are we clear?"

"Crystal."

"Good. So I'll see you tomorrow then. I look forward to it."

Stevie and Ray dropped me to the ground. A moment later, I heard the Cadillac start up and drive off. I laid on the pavement for a good long time, hurting all over. The nap I'd been contemplating earlier didn't sound like such a bad idea now and I let myself drift off into the darkness that had been clawing at the edge of my senses.

CHAPTER 3

I woke up in the back of an ambulance. Once I'd come to that stellar conclusion, other smaller details started falling into place. There was a bandage taped down over my right eye. I was wearing an oxygen mask. I was strapped to a backboard and wearing a cervical collar. I wiggled my fingers and toes, just to be sure, and found them all in working order. Even though I hurt all over, it was a pain that stayed far away and distant. I mostly felt like someone had wrapped me in a big, fluffy blanket, which I presumed was probably due to a healthy dose of pain medication. God bless each and every one of those beautiful bastards.

A face appeared in my field of vision, though I couldn't make out much in the way of details since the proprietor of said face was shining one of those little penlights into my one open eye. Whatever he saw seemed to pacify him, and the light vanished.

"Mister Heywood, you're in an ambulance."

"I gathered," I croaked. My throat didn't hurt per se,

but my mouth was horribly dry. My tongue felt too thick, too heavy to really form words.

"Do you remember what happened to you?" the face, which I assumed belonged to a paramedic, asked.

I tried to nod and remembered I couldn't really move my head.

"Yeah."

"Can you tell me?"

"I got my ass kicked, right and proper."

"That's one way to put it. We're taking you to the hospital now. You're pretty beat up."

"Ya don't say."

"Well, you're in good hands. Nothing life threatening, but it's going to take a while to get you patched up. The police are probably going to want to talk to you as well."

"Can't wait," I said and closed my eyes. I didn't sleep, but I was perfectly content to let myself slip down into the comfortable delirium of the pain meds.

The next few hours at the hospital were, to put it mildly, a test of my patience. The pain medication was starting to wear thin and a barrage of aches and pains began assaulting my body, starting at my head and working their way over what I was sure was every last nerve ending and molecule that made up yours truly. Once they'd cleaned me up, put twelve stitches into my face and another three into the cut over my other eye, a doctor came in and asked me a battery of questions. Said questions included who I was, who the president was and what year it was. After that came the CT scan, a lot more waiting, and finally a diagnosis of a concussion and the suggestion that I stay overnight for observation. I refused, signed some forms, got a prescription for some more pharmaceutical magic, and was starting to get dressed when the detective came in.

Detective Thaddeus Watkins is the kind of guy who is probably still to this day reminding people about the game-winning touchdown he scored some twenty odd years ago. Forget the fact that he probably scored said touchdown playing peewee football when he was six. He was a stout guy, a few inches taller than me, with black hair that was giving way to steely gray around the temples. His suit, an off the rack gray number, only made him look tired and rumpled, as opposed to professional.

Watkins was also an insufferable dick. As such, it was my moral obligation to respond in kind at absolutely every given opportunity.

"You know, Heywood. I was thinking about you last night," he said, crossing his arms over his chest.

"Hey, to each his own, but I don't swing that way, chief," I said.

His eyes narrowed.

"You've been running game around here for a long time, Heywood. It's only a matter of time, I'll catch ya," he said, turning his nose up towards the ceiling.

"I don't know what you're talking about. I provide a legitimate service. It's not my fault you're not as open minded as the rest of us."

Watkins laughed.

"Séances and exorcisms?" he asked.

I shrugged and pulled my shirt on.

"There are more things on heaven and earth, than dreamt of in your philosophy, Watkins."

"The hell does that even mean?"

I shook my head.

"For Christ's sake, man, read a book," I said.

"What?"

"Nevermind."

"That's what I thought," he said, tempering the words with the kind of self-righteous smugness that only the terminally stupid can muster.

"Aren't you supposed to be asking me who kicked the shit out of me?" I asked, sitting on the edge of the bed to pull my shoes on.

"Oh. Yeah," he said, lacing his words with a heavy dose of false concern. "Mister Heywood, can you tell me anything about the individual who assaulted you?"

For a fraction of a second, I actually considered telling him the truth. I debated spelling out the whos and the whys in explicit detail. Then I remembered the picture of my old man that Waylon had waved in front of my face.

My Pop had had it rough enough over the past few months. I didn't need to make it any worse by getting him involved in my mess. If I ratted out the Carvers they'd involve him in a manner that suggested a few of Waylon's friends would pay him a visit. While I had no doubt that my old man could handle a few dime store thugs, he deserved better than that.

"No," I said.

"That's about what I figured," Watkins said.

I finished putting my shoes on and stood, which turned out to be a lot harder than I expected. The room started to tilt. I put a hand against the wall and took a few deep breaths, steadying myself. When I opened my eyes, Watkins was still blocking the doorway.

"You know, one day I'm gonna see you arrested, Heywood. If there's one thing I hate, it's someone running something on some hard-working folks, bilking them out of money they earned," he said. "You'll screw up, and I'll catch you. Bet on that, Buster."

Watkins grinned, letting me stew on that for a moment. Don't get me wrong: I wasn't intimidated. Not really. Mostly I just figured I was too damn pretty to go to jail. It didn't help that he was right, either. Lately, I'd been making it a habit to lift whatever valuables I could while I was performing my services. It was mostly little things, jewelry and the like, stuff that wouldn't be missed for a while. Still, it was a step up in the risk department, and one I probably shouldn't be taking.

"Are we done?" I asked, shrugging into my jacket. It was an old black leather biker jacket that had belonged to my father back when he used to ride. It was meant to be body armor against road rash and as such, it weighed probably a good ten pounds. Given my current state, the damn thing almost pulled me down to the floor. Still, it was comforting.

"For the moment," Watkins said. He gave me a wide grin, winked, and I kid you not, did the finger gun thing. The depths of his douchebaggery were boundless. "See you soon, Heywood."

"God, I hope not," I said, watching him saunter out the door.

I sat down on the bed and started going through my pockets. I was patched up and in one piece. My head hurt, my ears were ringing, I ached in places I didn't know were acheable, and I wanted a drink so bad it was bordering on obsession, but I was in one piece. After a minute, I found my phone and the business card the woman from the bar had given me earlier. I dialed the number and slipped the card back into my pocket. I got up, limped over to the door, and shut it. The phone hadn't even rung before she answered it, her voice all condescension and weird accent.

"Mister Heywood," she said.

"Well, that's more than a little creepy," I said.

"Excuse me?"

"Nevermind. That offer you asked me about, is it still on the table?"

"It could be. Would you be willing to meet with me tomorrow morning?"

"Yeah, same place as earlier work for you?"

"Actually, no. I would prefer you sober. Are you familiar with World Coffee?"

"I am," I said.

"Good. Shall we say, eight o'clock tomorrow morning?"

"Can we say closer to noon?" I asked.

Silence answered me. I sighed.

"Fine. Eight it is," I said.

"Excellent," she said and hung up.

I made one more call on my way out of the hospital. Thankfully, some kind soul had thought to leave my cane in my room, or else I'd have been hard pressed to stay upright and mobile for the walk out of the emergency room. As it was, even with the cane, it was still a bit treacherous trying to dodge doctors, nurses, patients, and janitors with a head clouded with pain medication. My brain still felt a bit like jelly and I wasn't entirely steady on my feet. Thankfully, the temperature outside had dropped and the cold air was like a slap in the face, bringing some clarity back to my senses.

Sam pulled up a few minutes later and got out of the car, jogging over to help me. I figured that probably said everything I needed to know about what kind of shape I was in, and more than that what kind of a person Sam was. He wore his standard fare, jeans and a plain gray hooded sweatshirt. In a lot of ways he still reminded me of the homeless street kid I'd met five years ago. Since then he'd completely turned his life around. He'd pulled himself up from sleeping under bridges and in back alleys to owning a sort of rec-center-slash-boxing-gym-slash-outreach-slash-community-center for homeless LGBT teens. He put them up when they needed a place to crash, had programs to help them find jobs, places to live, kick drugs, and he taught them how to defend themselves. He regarded the kids that came through his doors as his own and for what it was worth, I was pretty sure he remembered the name of each and every last one of them.

I understood why he did it. A few years ago, he'd been one of those kids he was helping now, put out on the street after his own father had discovered he was gay.

"What the hell happened to you?" Sam asked, helping me into the passenger seat of a little Japanese sedan.

I explained what had happened after I left Jack in the Wood, but left out the part about the woman and her job offer. Sam didn't exactly approve of how I made a living. He didn't judge me for it or hold it against me, but he wasn't exactly a fan. As such, I didn't see a need to purvey that little tidbit of information.

"Jesus, what the hell were you thinking, borrowing money from them?"

I shrugged.

"I needed it."

"More than you need, I don't know, your life?"

I gave him a flat stare. He didn't flinch. After a moment, I turned my attention back to the road. Sam drove for a few minutes in silence.

"So, where am I taking you?" Sam asked.

"About that. Is there any way you could crash at my place tonight? I'm not supposed to sleep or something," I said. "Concussion and all."

"Nope," Sam said. "You can rest on the couch at the gym, though. I have a shit ton of paper work to do for this new grant I'm trying to land. Besides, I'm pretty sure Andy would kill me if I brought you back to my house. He's still pretty pissed with you."

"Right," I said.

"Besides, your place smells like sweat and stale beer," Sam added. "Couch or nothing."

"I appreciate it," I said. It wasn't my own bed, but it was better than not waking up due to coma or some such nonsense. "What's Andy got against me, any way?"

Sam pulled to a stop at a red light and turned towards me.

"Seriously? Need I remind you about the weekend his sister came to visit? The tequila? The video camera?"

"Oh," I said. "Yeah. Forgot about that."

"Yeah, he hasn't."

CHAPTER 4

I didn't get much rest at Sam's place. It's not that the couch wasn't comfortable, it's just hard to sleep somewhere that isn't my own bed.

Truth be told, I also felt a little guilty, laying there, riding out my morphine and wishing I had a drink while anti-drug and safe sex posters stared at me from every wall. Sam took my bad attitude in stride. He popped out of his office to check on me every hour or so, made sure I had a cold bottle of water within easy reach, and all in all acted like the kind of friend that I probably didn't deserve.

Sam dropped me off at my truck at roughly half past seven the next morning. It warmed my heart to see my truck still sitting there, that some asshole hadn't had her towed, or worse, vandalized her.

"It's okay sweetheart, daddy's here," I said, running my hand along the hood.

I unlocked the door, climbed in, leaned over the bench seat, and fished my flask out from its hiding place in the glove box, underneath the stacks of napkins, ketchup packets, and the little fake leather folder that held my registration. It took me a minute to get the flask open, given that my hands were shaking from the cold air and complete lack of sleep. I started the engine, clicked the heat over to full, took a long swig from the flask, and then settled back into the seat while the interior got nice and toasty. Not that the drive to World Coffee was far, but I needed a little comfort after the night I'd had. I figured I'd earned it. I took another pull off the flask, then twisted the cap back on and slipped it into my coat. I had to admit, I was already starting to feel better, more centered, maybe even a little, dare I say it, Zen.

Along with World Coffee, the Flatiron Building also housed everything from therapists to "sustainability engineers," whatever the hell that was. To me, the entire structure looked like it would've been more at home in New York with its cousin, maybe in Hell's Kitchen or the Bronx. It just always felt out of place in Asheville.

My future employer had already commandeered one of the small tables that sat outside. She'd already ordered, and two mugs sat billowing steam in the center of the table, next to a small plate of pastries and a little carafe that I guessed held more coffee. She saw me and gestured to the seat across from her.

I made my way over and sat down, setting my cane on the edge of the table. She eyed the bruises on my face.

And the stitches.

And the bandage that covered the majority of the right side of my face.

"I see you had an eventful evening," she said, nodding towards the cup. "Coffee?"

"Thanks," I said, picking up one of the cups and taking a slow, cautious sip. The coffee was delicious and just shy of being the same temperature as molten rock.

"I ordered some Danishes as well, if you'd like one."

I answered by picking one up, taking a bite that was large enough to be considered rude in most polite social circles, and washed it down with another mouthful of coffee. I kept this up with a silent satisfaction and more than a bit of gluttonous joy, until both the coffee and the Danish were gone.

"So, job's still on the table then?" I asked.

"It is."

"Twenty thousand?"

"No."

"No?"

"No."

"What the hell do you mean, no?" I asked, leaning forward in my chair.

"I mean that the terms of the offer no longer involve a payment of twenty thousand dollars," she said, picking her own coffee cup up and taking a small sip. "That was yesterday's offer. Today's offer is five thousand."

"You've got to be fucking kidding me," I said. I picked up the coffee cup, noticed it was empty, and dropped it back on the table a little harder than I intended.

"Actually, I'm not," she said.

I turned my options over in my head, tracing my thumb over the rim of the coffee cup in front of me. To be fair, there wasn't a whole lot in the way of options to be considered. I either found a way to come up with some of the cash to pay off Waylon and his brother, or I receive another ass kicking of epic, and quite possibly fatal, proportions. Worse, they'd go after my old man. Which was a situation that wouldn't go well for one, or both, of the parties involved.

"Fine," I said finally. "But I want half up front."

The woman kept her eyes locked on me and plucked a small piece off of one of the Danishes. She put it in her mouth, chewing it slowly.

"That's acceptable," she said, finally. "If you give me your word."

"My word? Seriously?"

"An oath, actually."

"Right. And how does that work, per se?"

"Simple. You lick the palm of your hand. I will do the same. We'll shake hands, and you will swear by the blood of your kin that you will retrieve the stone. When that is done, I will tell you everything you need to know to retrieve the stone."

"You're serious?" I asked, incredulous.

"Very."

I watched her for a moment, wondering if maybe this was all some sort of prank or joke.

"Fine. I'll bite," I said.

The woman nodded.

"Go on," she said.

So I did as she asked. In the middle of the cafe, in front of God and everyone, I licked my hand from palm to fingertips and stuck it out across the table. She did the same, and took my hand in hers. It was a little gross and all kinds of strange, but a guy's got to eat.

"Repeat after me," she said. "On my kin, I make this oath, and bind myself to it."

I repeated the words, and for the briefest of instances, my entire body was hit by a wave of arctic-like cold. It came and went so fast that, even now, still shivering, I wasn't sure it had actually happened.

"It's done," she said.

"Well, now that we've officially traded spit, mind telling me your name?" I asked.

"My name is Abigail Lysone."

"What is that? French?" I asked.

"I suppose that's close enough."

"Alright," I said. "Give me the deets."

"Deets?"

"Details," I said, refilling my cup. "Tell me about this, what was it again?"

"Ledberg Runestone."

"Right, tell me about the stone," I said, sitting back and sipping at my coffee.

"The Ledberg Runestone was discovered—"

I held up a hand, cutting her off.

"The things I need to know if I'm going to acquire said stone for you. That's what I need, not a history lesson," I said. Maybe it was the repeated blows to the head, the lack of sleep, or the fact that I was here roughly four hours before I'm usually even awake, but I was feeling a little punchier than usual.

"Very well, straight to the point, then," she said. If she was put off by my tone, she didn't show it. "The fragment of the stone was stolen from my husband some time ago. Fortunately, it has recently resurfaced, here, in Asheville."

"Where, exactly?"

"Of that, I am unsure. I simply have it from a reliable source that it is within the city. Besides, if I knew where it was, I wouldn't have to pay you to find it."

"Touché."

"May I continue?"

I took another sip of coffee and kept my mouth shut.

"The fragment is roughly the size of a large, hardcover book and, much like its parent, displays a pictorial carving of the battle of Ragnarok," she said, her accent giving an odd inflection to the traditional name for the Norse apocalypse. "It also has certain, shall we say, inherent properties."

"Inherent properties? How about we elaborate on that," I said.

"Well, like anything which has had centuries of belief heaped upon it, it is an object of power. Perhaps not as substantial as the Ark of the Covenant, or the Shroud of Turin, but power nonetheless."

I turned that over in my noodle for a minute. Everything in the world has at least some measure of innate power, call it magic, chi, energy, whatever, it was a universal constant. Certain people, like myself, can tap into that power. Granted, there are limits on what people with the necessary talent can derive that power from. In my case, I was what most people would call a shaman or medicine man. I tapped into the energy inherent in nature, primarily plants, herbs, and stones. It was only one of my many talents.

Power though, power comes with a price.

For example, witches dealt in fate. They could manipulate it, twist it, the works. I'd never actually met one, but the scuttlebutt was that witches could see how fate worked, and in some cases, manipulate those threads to their own ends. In the end, or so I'm told, that sort of power drove most of them about nine different kinds of stark raving mad. In my case, I had to use my blood as a catalyst. There are other parts to my powers, sure, but in the end, it all comes down to the blood.

The power of faith—that was a different animal altogether. I didn't really have any idea how it worked and only the truly devout could really put it to use anyway. However, when someone could tap into it, the results ranged from miraculous to absolutely terrifying. Couple that sort of potential with an item that has, over time, become a sort of battery for the power religious devotion generates, and you get an item that's the magical equivalent of a nuclear warhead. Sure, you could do a lot of good with something like that. You could also level a city with that much mojo. It was why the church was so big on hanging onto bits and pieces of dead saints.

"Alright, that begs my next question," I said, finally.

"Go ahead."

"What exactly are you planning on doing with said stone?" I asked.

"Am I asking you what you're planning on doing with the money I pay you?"

"Be that as it may, the question still warrants asking."

"Perhaps," she said with a slight shrug. "Mister Heywood, I'm paying you to find and retrieve this item for me. Not ask me stupid questions. What I'm doing with it isn't your concern. Judging from the state of your face and the fact that you called me not more than twenty-four hours after I made my initial offer, I'm assuming we wouldn't be having this conversation unless you desperately needed the money. Now, I'm going to go on the assumption that your already shaky moral compass isn't going to be a problem and you can get to work," she said, her words clipped with irritation.

I glared at her over the rim of my coffee cup. She met my gaze with eyes that were the color of glacial ice and just as cold. Something about this whole deal had me on edge. She was right, however. I was desperate.

I set the cup on the table, pushing it slowly to the center. "I guess I'm on the clock," I said.

Lysone offered me a chilly smile and reached into her coat, withdrawing a white envelope, stretched thick with cash. She set it on the table and slid it over to me. I picked it up and peeked inside long enough to see a stack of bills, before sliding it into my jacket pocket. I stood up, grabbing my cane off of the table.

"Mister Heywood?" she asked as I was turning to leave.

"Yeah?"

"You are aware that if you try to renege on this deal, or screw me over, I'll see to it that your leg and the beating you took last night are the least of your worries, correct?"

I stared at her for a long moment. It wasn't so much what she said, it was how she said it. There wasn't the slightest bit of hesitation in her voice. As far as she was concerned, this was a universal truth on par with Newtonian law.

"I suppose I am now," I said.

"Very good. I expect to hear from you tomorrow with an update."

I took my flask out of my pocket, opened it and took a sip, then tipped it towards her.

"Cheers."

I finished off the last of the booze once I'd gotten back in my truck. I put the empty flask in the glove box and pulled the envelope out of my pocket. Counting the money in front of Lysone would have been rude, but I was damn sure going to check that she paid me what she'd agreed to. It was all there, two grand in hundreds and another five hundred in twenties. I put the twenties into the pocket of my jeans and set the rest of the money on the seat beside me, started the truck, and threw it into gear.

First stop, refill. After that, pay the Carvers and get them off my ass.

Once those two things were done, it was time to go work.

Life, after all, was all about priorities.

CHAPTER 5

The Carvers owned a bar called The Poor Confederate in Black Mountain, a small suburb about twenty minutes outside of Asheville. It was one of those hole-in-the-wall dive bars. Like *Cheers*, but with a lot more Merle Haggard and violence. The building itself was nothing more than a red brick cube with grimy windows and neon beer signs, offset by a gravel lot and located next to a strip of shops and a grocery store. There were a few trucks parked outside, mostly old beaters and work trucks laden down with everything from lumber to scrap metal to baying hunting dogs in metal boxes. I parked as close to the door as I could get and got out of the truck. Overhead, storm clouds were starting to gather and a steady wind was starting to kick up, dust and trash dancing across the little gravel lot.

The inside of the Poor Confederate wasn't much better looking than the exterior. If anything, the outside was a touch of class compared to the squalor inside. The lighting was dim and the entire place smelled of spilled beer, sweat, and shame. The floor was marred and stained wood. If I had to guess, I'd say the majority of the stains were either puke or blood, probably both. Centerfolds from porn magazines lined the wall behind the bar. Given the amount and size of the hair on the models, I put them as being from sometime between Woodstock and the birth of disco. A ratty pool table sat in a back corner. A few tables with mismatched chairs lined the wall opposite the bar. The jukebox, which was old enough to still play records, was next to the door and featured the likes of George Jones, all three Hanks, Skynyrd, and of course, David Allan Coe.

A few locals were sitting at the bar. They were mostly working-class types who, much like yours truly, preferred to drink their breakfast. They gave me a cursory glance as I came in, then turned their attention back to their beers. I made my way over to the bar, finding a spot as far from them as I could, and slid up onto a stool.

Melly, the bartender, came over and set a beer down in front of me. I have to admit, I had a touch of a thing for Melly. She had the slim, toned build one usually saw on a dancer, all dainty and perfect, built for graceful motion. She wore her hair, which almost touched the small of her back, loose and covering one side of her face, the dark chestnut of her natural color mixing with the dyed in streaks of blood red and a green like old money.

"You look like you need this," she said.

I nodded and reached for my pocket.

"This one's on the house," she added.

Did I mention she had a saint-like sense of charity?

"Thanks," I said, taking a sip. So far, the whiskey was doing a good job of keeping the multitude of aches and pains at bay, but I wasn't opposed to giving it a bit of backup. "Cash or Waylon in?"

"Not yet. Should be here before noon," she said and set about wiping down the bar top. "They do that to your face?"

I looked down into my beer and didn't answer. Maybe it was my ego, but I didn't have it in me to tell her that I'd gotten my ass kicked by her bosses. She gave me a long look, sighed, and opted to let it go.

Like I said, saintly.

"How's your dad?" she asked.

"Better actually," I said. "The new shop is up and running, he's turning decent business."

"Good to hear," she said.

"Yeah, he's out of the red and into the black. Can't ask for much more than that."

"He fixed my transmission a few weeks ago. That damn car runs better than it has in years," she said.

"Sounds like him," I said.

We spent the next hour or so involved in idle chitchat, talking about family, friends, jobs, love life, the works. Turns out, Melly was single, which I filed away into my little mental notebook of things to investigate further when her bosses didn't want to kill me.

"You sure they're coming today, Melly?" I asked.

She looked at the clock over the bar, and shrugged.

"They said they were."

"Well, I don't have all day," I said, standing up. "Got a pen?"

She snatched a pen out of a small can next to the register and slid it over to me. I jotted my number down on a napkin and handed it, along with the pen, back to her.

"Give me a buzz when they show up?" I asked.

She nodded, slipping the napkin into her pocket. "Will do."

"You're a peach," I said.

"I know," she said and smiled. Suddenly the inside of this little hole looked a lot less bleak.

I was on my way to the door when it opened, bathing the bar in pale light. The rain had started outside, and even with the cloud cover and rainfall, it was so dim in the Poor Confederate that the little bit of light that slipped through the door was enough to make me shield my eyes. I looked back up in time to see Waylon and Cash saunter in, and like a couple of hungry sharks, they instantly set in on me.

"Well, shit the bed! What have we here? Jonah Heywood, as I live and breathe," Waylon said, clapping a ginormous hand on my shoulder.

Cash, on the other hand, just cleared his throat and licked his lips.

"So what can we do you for, Jonah?" Waylon said.

"Can we talk?" I asked.

"Of course, we're all friends here. Melly, bring us a round. We'll be in the office."

"Whatever you say, Waylon," Melly said, barely concealing the note of disgust in her voice.

I learned something in the body language that occurred between Melly and Waylon in that second or two that followed their exchange. First, Melly hated him. She hated him with a visceral intensity that was almost palpable. Waylon, on the other hand, viewed her as nothing more than property. The moment passed just as quickly as it had come, and Waylon plastered that big chummy grin back on his face.

"Jonah, follow me. Let's chat," Waylon said, throwing an arm over my shoulder and all but dragging me towards the booths at the back of the bar. Cash fell in step behind us. I could feel his gaze on the back of my neck and had to suppress a shudder.

Waylon led me to a booth in the back. I slid into the bench-style seat and he slid in beside me, blocking me off. Cash sat across from me, his eyes never leaving my face. Melly came over a moment later, carrying three frosted beer mugs in one hand and a pitcher of beer in the other. She set a mug in front of each of us, the pitcher in the center of the table, and then turned to retake her position at the bar.

Waylon watched her go back behind the bar with the same consideration he gave the bar stools, the tables, damn near everything inside of these four walls. If she knew he was staring, she didn't give any indication. She just took up her post behind the bar and went about with the business of polishing glasses before the afternoon crowd showed up.

"So, what is it you're wanting to talk about?" Waylon asked.

I took the envelope with the two grand out of my jacket and dropped it on the table, next to the pitcher. He picked it up and passed it to Cash, who counted it and handed it back.

"Two thousand," Cash said.

Waylon whistled.

"That's impressive, Heywood. Damned impressive. Not even a day's time and you show up on my doorstep with an envelope full of money. That's some motivation, I have to admit."

Waylon looked at his brother and an unspoken communication passed between them. Whatever it was, it made me nervous. Scratch that, it made me really, really nervous.

"Problem is, Jonah, that doesn't entirely bring you up to date."

I blinked.

"I'm sorry, come again?"

"You owe us ten thousand. Two missed payments and you know as well as I do, the interest gets tacked onto the principal. So, according to my calculations you owe us... how much is it again, Cash?"

"Fourteen thousand, four hundred dollars," Cash said in that serial killer monotone.

"The fuck are you talking about?" I snapped, my anger overriding my common sense.

"Now, Jonah, let's not get carried away. You agreed to the terms. Twenty points on the principal, interest gets paid before the principal. That was the deal and you're short two large and some change."

"That's bullshit," I said.

"No, that's business."

"Are you kidding me?" I said, one hand clenching the handle of my mug a little too hard. It took everything I had to keep from smashing him in the head with it.

Waylon held up a hand.

"Slow down there, chief. I'm a decent human being. You tried to make good and I can appreciate that. Now, here's what I'm going to do. I'll give you—I don't know. Cash, what do you think?"

"A day."

"Nah, let's say two," Waylon said. "Two days. Get me my money in two days and we'll be square. If you don't, well, I don't know how much clearer I can be with you. I'll probably have to go seek payment elsewhere."

I took the hint.

"If you go near my old man, Waylon, I'll kill you," I said. In that moment, I meant it.

Cash stood up. My hand tightened on the beer mug, the only weapon I had. Waylon held a hand up, meeting Cash's eyes. The tension leaked out of the younger Carver brother and he slid back down into the seat.

Waylon turned towards me. He wore a smug, arrogant grin.

"Jonah, I'm going to let that go. I get it, you're emotional. I'm a reasonable man, but let's be clear, if you ever threaten me again, well, I'm going to let Cash get up and I'm going to walk away."

He stood up.

"Now get the fuck out of my bar," he said.

I obliged him. Melly watched me go, her eyes darting between me and both Carver brothers.

Outside of the Poor Confederate, the rain had gone from a light drizzle to a torrential downpour. It summed up my mood perfectly. The rain, coupled with the chill in the air, made me feel tired and heavy and set a deep ache into my leg. I crossed the parking lot at what, for me at least, was a close approximation of a jog, and slid the key into the driver's side door lock.

I felt the rise of power in the air as I was opening the door. It didn't have the sudden, snapping tension of a spell.

This was something entirely different. It was more of a presence. A very strong, scary presence and it wasn't even close to human.

CHAPTER 6

I turned around as slowly and non-threateningly as possible, just in case the owner of said presence was of the face-eating persuasion. The woman, who looked like she was barely old enough to vote, stood at the far edge of the small parking lot. Like me, she was drenched to the bone, blonde hair hanging in loose, lanky strands around her face. She wore jeans that consisted of more rips than denim and a Mötley Crüe T-shirt, cut short enough to show a flat plane of stomach. Her eyeliner was smeared, giving her eyes a dark, shadowed look.

We stood there in the rain, getting soaked to the bone and staring at each other.

When she finally did move, it was at a slow, purposeful stride. The closer she got, the more I wanted to jump inside my truck and hide. There was something about her that scared the absolute piss out of me in a way that Waylon and his brother couldn't come close to.

She stopped maybe six inches away from me, close

enough that, despite the rain, I could smell her shampoo, or perfume radiating off of her. It was odd. I couldn't place the smell, but it made me think of flowers growing in snow.

"It is you," she said, finally.

"Uh, yeah?"

She reached out, her fingertips ever so lightly dancing across my cheek. It made me shiver. I didn't know what the hell this woman was, and I damned sure wasn't about to open up my senses to view her aura. I had a terrifying feeling that it would be like staring into the sun.

"You have to stop her," she said.

"I, what?"

"You have to stop her," she repeated.

"I take it you mean Lysone?"

"You have to get what she wants and you have to stop her."

"Lady, what the in the bloody blue hell are you talking about?" I asked, taking a step back. I'd had my fair share of irritation for one day. All I wanted to do was get in my truck, have a drink, and get on with finding this stupid rock. Instead, I'd already had to deal with death threats, loan sharks, and now, to top it all off, this special kind of crazy.

It wasn't even noon yet.

"You don't understand all the things tied to you, all the paths you must travel to make this right," she said.

I took another step back and the girl's hand shot out, wrapping around my wrist. She may have weighed a total of ninety pounds, but she had a grip that would put Waylon to shame.

It felt like an electrical current shot up my arm as the

girl's eyes turned white. The color, which was a pale sky blue, drained out, as did the black of her pupils.

I tried to jerk my hand back, to break her grip, and found that I was severely lacking in the strength department. That same fear I'd felt initially ramped up a notch. I started jerking my arm back, trying to break her grip.

It was at that point that she chose to let go. I fell backwards, directly into a puddle.

"Oh, for crying out loud," I growled, picking my cane up out of the gravel and struggling back to my feet. "Look lady, I don't know what the hell your problem is, but I'm done. I'm out. Deuces."

"No, you're not done at all. Not in the slightest. You've started to play her game, and now you're dancing," she said, and turned a pirouette right in the middle of the parking lot. "And you'll dance, just like she wants you to, unless you change the rules. You have to change the rules."

The girl positioned herself between me and my truck, blocking my path. She let her arms hang limp at her sides and tilted her head.

"You really don't see it do you? What you've started? What you're doing?"

"Obviously not."

"Then you're not looking in the right places, are you?"

I stood there, soaking wet, irritated, and more than a little pissed off. She wasn't going to let me leave, at least not yet. That much was obvious.

"So where exactly are the right places, then? I'd really like to wrap this up so I can leave."

She shook her head.

"Not here."

"C'mon, give me something. Work with me here."

"Oh no, I can't give you anything. You're already going to take on so much."

"What am I going to take on then, exactly?" I asked.

"Something you shouldn't. Something you should leave alone."

"You mean the stone?" I asked.

"No, not the stone. A key. For a lock. A big lock."

"Okay, I'll bite. So what does the key unlock then?"

"A big, big lock."

I closed my eyes and pinched the bridge of my nose. If the little twinge I felt in my temples at the moment was any indication of the headache I had rolling in, then before it was all said and done it was going to be one hell of a migraine.

"What does the lock, uh lock?" I asked, spacing out my words like I was talking to a small child.

"You tell me," she said.

I gaped at her. That was just about all I could handle from this terrifying tween.

"And I'm done."

I started towards the front of my truck. I was keen on the idea of getting out of the rain and getting my hands on a little something to warm my guts. I slowed down as I got close to her, just in case she tried anything, but she stepped aside and let me pass. I had the door open when she put a surprisingly light hand on my shoulder. I turned around.

"Jonah. You need to stop her," she said, sounding surprisingly lucid all of a sudden.

"Stop what, exactly?"

"You can't let her use it," she said, her hand moving

from my shoulder to touch my cheek again. She pushed a little bit of hair behind my ear. I used my cane to push her hand away, albeit gently. I didn't want to encourage her to try and break my neck or anything by moving too fast.

"Look, I have no idea what you're talking about, lady. It's cold. It's pouring rain. Unless you're about to impart some Yoda-like wisdom on me, we're done here," I said.

After another moment of silence on her end, I turned and got into my truck. She took a step back so I could close the door.

She was still standing there, watching me while I backed out of the lot and onto the street.

CHAPTER 7

I spent most of the drive back to Asheville shaking off the lingering fear from my meeting with, well, whoever she was. I was pretty sure she had been alluding to the stone that Lysone wanted me to find, but at the moment I had bigger fish to fry. It was already close to one in the afternoon, which left me with roughly twenty hours to find this hunk of rock, acquire it, return it, get paid, and still somehow scrounge up another several thousand dollars with which to pay off Waylon and Cash.

My life, I tell you. It's some kind of stellar.

As far as Asheville went, there was, at best, a miniscule portion of the mundane community that was in the know when it came to the supernatural. Those that knew a little something about something did their best to keep it quiet. Outside of a few factions—your vampires, werewolves, and Fae types—the majority of the ones in the know weren't much more than dabblers. We're talking your hippy wiccans, book store sorcerers, the occasional satanist, a few wannabe psychics, tarot card readers, conjure men, and every once in a while, some curious shmuck with a genuine academic interest. The mundanes that didn't run in the same circles I did were perfectly content to ignore anything strange, pretend it didn't happen, or just rationalize it away. After all, it's a lot easier to tell the folks around the water cooler that the shape you saw crouched over the homeless guy in the alley was just another homeless guy instead of say, a vampire looking for a late-night snack, or a Fae in the midst of one of their deals, most of which involved a mark giving up their first born in exchange for power, money, sex, or any other number of vices they felt the urge to indulge in.

What I needed right now was someone who was in the know when it came to the things that went bump in the night. Thankfully, that person actually owed me a favor, and not vice versa for a change. Bonus: I knew exactly where to find him.

I swung by my trailer, which, as far as homes go, wasn't much more than a metal box situated under a willow tree in the back corner of the Shady View Trailer park. I took a couple of hours to eat, change my bandages, rest up and put on a fresh, dry set of clothes. Thankfully, there was enough ointment smeared over my sutures that between that and the bandages, they hadn't really gotten wet. Once I'd made myself as presentable as I could be after the day I'd had I made the drive to Abandon.

Thirty minutes later I was parked in the small lot across the street, watching what was essentially the United Nations for Asheville's nastier denizens. This was where the vampires came to play their politics or pick up potential thralls, the Unseelie Fae came to indulge whatever appetite so moved them at the moment, and any other number of nasty things did their business. Namely, it was because Abandon was safe. They all considered this place as a sort of neutral ground, and as such, they were free to do their thing as long as they kept it nice and civil, though nice and civil has a whole different meaning when it involves a room full of monsters.

At first glance, Abandon looked like nothing more than an empty, derelict warehouse set in the middle of a bunch of other empty, derelict warehouses. That was, however, exactly what they wanted you to think. I'd looked in the joint before, a long time ago, without the mental walls in place that I use to block out the spirit world. What was underneath the illusion of the abandoned warehouse was, in truth, an opulent house. This place was about ten miles past expensive. It was three stories tall, the front surrounded by massive marble pillars wrapped in ivy. Statuary of various mythological figures lined the sidewalk under the guise of trashcans and streetlights. It was the infamous Faerie illusion magic of glamour at its finest and running at full power.

Once the rain slowed down enough that I wouldn't be forced to swim to make it across the street, I got out of my truck and made a shambling run for the entrance. Abandon didn't need bouncers. There was an enchantment on the place. If the owner, who was an absolute nightmare in his own right, didn't want you here, you didn't come in. It was as simple as that. You walked through the door and found yourself in the building next door, or down the street, or across town, or God knew where. I wasn't exactly sure where I stood with him, so I closed my eyes, took a deep breath and walked through the unmarked steel door that served as the entrance.

Everything went black and I felt like I'd walked into Saran wrap, like the air itself became tactile and elastic. For a moment, no longer than a breath, I felt weightless.

No matter how many times I came here, stepping into the club proper always threw me off. I knew full well that I should be standing in the husk of some factory from days gone by and not in what was essentially the world's strangest aviary. Ferns and flowers of all colors lined marble paths roughly as wide as city streets. Exotic bushes had been grown and shaped into booths. The paths opened onto a large dance floor, in the center of which was a massive ash tree, its branches reaching from wall to wall. The leaves alone were the size of hubcaps. Its upper branches stretched out and created a ceiling overhead, through which the twinkle of stars could be seen. An occasional butterfly drifted by and birds could be heard singing high up in the tree. Music, something medieval-sounding, with just a bit of a modern electronic vibe, seemed to come from everywhere at once.

People were scattered about, some dressed, more in various states of undress. There were couples at tables, lines of white powder drawn out on massive leaves or flower petals, some with straws, some with syringes. I could pick out the Fae among the crowd. They were beautiful, startlingly perfect creatures of alien grace and sensuality. Security looked more like the massive bruisers that you'd expect to read about living under bridges or in caves. I saw a few other supernatural types scattered amongst the crowd, vampires mostly. They were the easiest to spot given that most of them looked diseased, veins showing through their pale skin, eyes and teeth yellowed. The fact that, regardless of gender, they didn't have any hair, helped make them a little easier to pick out, too.

It took me a few minutes to survey the crowd, but I found whom I was searching for at the back corner of the dance floor, leaning against a booth. I picked my way through the throng, which, with a cane, was a lot harder than it looked. Just being in this place lit up every base desire you can imagine, and very attractive women in very little clothing motioned me over and whispered something in my ear as I passed. The three-minute walk felt closer to twenty.

Penny was Abandon's resident Doctor Feelgood, selling everything from prescription pain pills to crystal meth, all the way up to drugs that were only identified by a string of numbers and letters. He was average height, a little on the thin side, and tended to dress loudly. Tonight it was lime-green slacks and a blue-and-red Hawaiian shirt. His hair was an obnoxiously bright copper.

I sauntered over and took a spot next to him.

"Penny," I said, waiting to interject until after he had passed off a small baggie of white powder to a customer.

"Jonah, been a minute since you've been up in here. Should I take it that means you're not here on a social call?"

I didn't answer.

"That's what I thought," he said. "I'm guessing you're not looking for party favors?"

"Nope."

"Looking to hear the word on the street then, huh?" he asked.

"Yep."

Penny nodded. In a lot of ways being a drug dealer in a club was a lot like being a janitor at the CIA. You were a part of the scenery. People talked openly around you because, as far as they were concerned, you were inconsequential. You were the help. Once you did what was needed of you, you ceased to exist. In turn, this meant you overhead a lot of things that people probably didn't want overheard. Things that, to the right person, could be valuable. Penny was smart and spun the information game into a pretty lucrative side racket. It would probably get him killed, but hey, beggars and choosers and all that.

"Alright, lay it on me."

"A runestone, or rather, a piece of one. Word on the playground is that it's popped up local. I need to know who has it."

"I might have heard something," Penny said. "What's it worth?"

"A clean slate?"

Penny nodded, mulling that over for a minute. A few years ago, he wasn't much more than a corner dealer when a rather nasty street gang, the Voodoo Kings had moved in. They were intent on making a name for themselves and, as such, had started taking out their competition. Big difference between them and the other bands of hoodlums running around the streets. The Kings, instead of using guns, would use some good old fashion black magic and craft a rep for themselves that put them at the top of the food chain. In the process, they cursed Penny. I'd intervened and he'd paid me pretty well as a result. Part of said payment was the promise of a favor.

"Yeah, alright," Penny said, finally. "It's not a lot. May not even have anything to do with what you're looking for."

"Lay it on me."

"Boss man shut the place down last night for a meeting."

"Yeah? With who?"

"Honestly?"

"No, lie to me," I said.

"I'm pretty sure it was Mama Duvalier."

I quirked a brow. Mama Duvalier was something of a mystery around Asheville. A lot of people had heard of her, even folks outside of the supernatural circles, but no one really knew her. She was equal parts myth, folk hero, and local legend. My mentor, Gretchen, had mentioned her a few times before she passed away a few years ago. The vibe I got was that there wasn't a lot of love lost between the two, but there was a ton of respect. I didn't know much more about her outside of what the rumor mill churned out, but word was that she and her family had a spot on a mountain this side of Maggie Valley and were involved in some pretty dark shit. I knew the general location, but not the exact address. That being said, I was pretty sure could find it if need be.

"What happened exactly?"

"She showed up, they cleared the joint out. I mean everyone. I hung around outside for a while, in case they opened back up. She came with a posse, all women. They stayed for about an hour, she left, and from what I saw she took a few extra heavies with her."

"No shit," I said.

If Mama Duvalier herself had come out, with the family, no less, it meant something big was going down. It was also the best lead I had in regards to the stone.

"God honest," Penny said. "That tell you anything?"

"We'll see," I said.

"Word. I need to get back to business, you mind?"

I shook my head and gave Penny a mock salute. As soon as I'd gotten a few steps away from him, a customer had already come to take my place. I fought my way through the crowd, once again fighting the temptation to stop and indulge in the various sundries on display and made my way towards the exit.

Outside, the rain had become a light mist. Mixed with the cold, it cast the streets in a dreary haze that clung to the skin. I took my time getting to my truck, despite the weather, and started trying to see if the new piece of intel I'd picked up fit in with everything else. Lysone had come to me yesterday, the same day that Mama Duvalier had come to Abandon. My gut told me the two lined up some-how. It was also a pretty safe assumption that this chunk of rock was much more powerful than Lysone had let on.

If I hadn't been lost in thought, I may have seen the attack coming. I also might have been aware of the disturb-ing uptick in ass-kickings I was receiving in parking lots lately. When the man stepped out of the mist, grabbed me by the shoulder, and launched me a good ten feet through the air one handed, I was caught completely off guard.

CHAPTER 8

When I hit the ground, it was on a small stretch of grass that separated the parking lot and the sidewalk. All things considered, I could have found a lot worse places to land at bone-jarring velocities. Though, at this point, I was starting to get a little frustrated with how my day was going.

I lay there in the wet grass in clothes I'd changed into less than two hours ago, sucking in the cold and the damp. I'll be the first to admit that I'm not exactly a scrapper. I am, however, a sneaky little bastard when I have to be.

I waited until I saw my assailant's boot come into my field of vision and hooked it with my cane, yanking his leg out from underneath him. Whoever he was, he went down hard. I didn't wait for him to try and get up. I swung the cane as hard as I could, right into my assailant's yarbles.

My attacker made a sound that was somewhere between a growl and a squeak, both hands instantly covering his junk.

I got my feet under me and stood up. Now that I could

actually see the guy, it dawned on me just how damned big he was. He made Waylon look small. He was seven feet tall with pale eyes and shoulder-length blond hair. He wore jeans and a plain black t-shirt, the fabric of which was stretched across a chest roughly the width of a small car. He had a beard, cut short, save for two long braids hanging down from his chin. He was already recovering, pulling himself to a seated position. I took two steps and swung my cane again, hitting him across the bridge of his nose. There was an audible crunch and a torrent of blood started pouring down over his beard.

I wasn't sure if he had much fight left in him, and I wasn't entirely keen on sticking around and finding out. So I turned tail and hobbled back to my truck. I made it into the cab just as he was getting back to his feet, the entire lower half of his face hidden beneath a curtain of blood. Given that he was smiling, I'd seen just about everything I needed to confirm that in this case, cowardice was the better part of valor.

I started the truck and slammed it into gear, flooring the gas. The tires squealed for a split second before they caught traction on the wet asphalt and sent me fishtailing through the parking lot. The big guy, who or whatever he was, got to his feet and started after me in a long, loping run. He was on an intercept course. I was in two thousand pounds of good old-fashioned American steel. If he wanted to play chicken, I was more than happy to oblige him.

I stomped the gas, sending the truck squealing forward. My assailant, seeing my intent, adjusted his course and a second later, lowered his shoulder, driving it into the side of my truck. He hit hard enough to rock me up onto two wheels and send me sliding a good ten feet across the wet blacktop.

When my tires caught again, I was on the sideways street, and fighting to straighten the wheel and get my truck back under control before I took out a few streetlights, and tore off through the streets of Asheville. I drove like that for a good five minutes, seething that he'd hurt my girl, completely ignoring speed limits, red lights, and praying that Asheville's finest had better things to do on a weekday night than be on the lookout for half-inebriated speeders running for their lives from marauding giants.

By the time I pulled myself together and the adrenaline had started fading, Abandon was a long way into my rear view. I pulled over and took a moment to breathe. My hands were shaking and the coppery taste of adrenaline filled my mouth. I pulled the bottle out from under my seat and took a long pull, letting the booze warm my gut and calm my nerves. I sat there for another minute and took a few more swallows from the bottle when my phone rang and shot another round of adrenaline into my system.

"Jesus Christ!" I shouted on reflex.

I picked it up and checked the number. I didn't recognize it.

"Yeah? Hello?"

"Jonah? It's Melly. I need your help."

"Uh, okay?" I said, checking my face in the rear view. My bandages were gone, exposing the stitches. I reached up, lightly touching them with my finger. It came away shiny with antibacterial ointment.

"Can you pick me up?" she asked, voice quivering between rage and tears.

"Hold on, what happened?" I asked.

"Please, just pick me up."

"Alright, alright. Where are you?"

"I can meet you outside of Izzy's in ten minutes. Can you do that?"

I knew the place she was talking. Izzy's coffeehouse was a far cry from where I'd met Lysone, and was a lot more my speed.

"Yeah, I can be there."

"Good," she said and paused for a breath. "Thank you," she added before hanging up the phone. I stared at it for a long moment then tossed it on the dashboard. I took another drink, shoved the bottle back under the seat, and then pulled away from the curb and back into the mostly nonexistent traffic.

Melly was standing on the sidewalk just outside of Izzy's when I pulled up. She was wearing jeans and a hooded sweatshirt, the hood up, strands of her hair falling in front of her face. She had her arms crossed over her chest and kept pacing a step or two in each direction before reversing course. She kept her eyes on the street. When she saw me pull up she hurried over to the passenger side door. I leaned over, unlocking it.

"Thanks. I guess I owe you one," she said, sliding up into the passenger seat and shutting the door.

"Don't mention it," I said, "where to?"

"I don't know," she said. "Just drive."

I turned towards her. She was on the edge of the seat, pressed against the door, watching the street.

"Ooookay," I said. "Anything you'd like to share?"

She didn't answer. Finally, I shrugged, put my truck

in gear, and pulled out. We drove like that for the next ten minutes, neither of us saying anything and rolling along with no destination in mind. She kept the hood up, chewing absently at her thumb as I drove.

"So, you want to tell me what's going on?" I asked, finally.

She turned towards me, sliding the hood back from her face. Her left cheek was swollen along the jawline, the normally pale skin already turning an angry purple.

"Jesus," I said. "The hell happened to you?"

"Cash happened to me," she said, turning her attention back to the passing scenery outside the window.

"Carver? Cash Carver? He did that?"

"Yeah," she said.

"You should see him," she added with a weak smile.

"Tell me what happened," I said, "and how I can help."

Melly let out a long, slow sigh. Whatever had happened, it was obvious she wasn't up for talking about it. She was putting up a strong front, but the way she kept looking out the window scanning the sidewalk, the other cars, said something serious had gone down. Whatever it was, it was something more than just a bruise on her cheek.

"I need a place to stay for a day or two, at least until I figure something else out. Somewhere I don't have to worry about Cash finding me. I didn't want to take my car, just in case."

"I get that."

"Do you know somewhere? A hotel maybe?"

"I can do you one better," I said.

Melly looked at me for a long second, one thin brow lifted.

"Don't get any ideas, Heywood."

"That's not what I meant. I know a place you can stay," I said, hoping that the warmth in my cheeks didn't translate to color.

"Seriously?"

"Yep, and I'll pay dearly for it."

CHAPTER 9

We drove in silence, and while this whole situation bothered me, I didn't want to push on Melly and dig for the
details that she wasn't ready to give. She looked like she'd
been through enough without me badgering her. Instead,
I played with the radio until I found the soothing tones of
Zeppelin, Kansas, and BTO, and drove out of town to a
small, one-story house in an equally small neighborhood
about a mile off Lake Lure.

The house, while older than most of the ones surrounding it, was in perfect repair and while not exactly
cheery-looking from the outside, was cozy enough. Every
shingle, painted the color of storm clouds, was in its place.
The shutters on the two street-facing windows were a pris-
tine, and equally spotless, white. A single cedar tree stood
in a perfectly maintained front yard, a circle around its base
filled with purple and white irises. The blue flickering light
of a TV played across the window, flashing to white, then

red. I parked across the street from the house and killed the engine, listening to it quietly tick.

"And where are we exactly?" Melly asked, climbing out of the cab and coming around to the driver's side.

"My old man's house."

"Oh," she said. "And how is he going to feel about you bringing strange girls home in the middle of the night?"

"I'm hoping he feels better about it now than he did when I was a teenager."

Melly snickered.

"Lead the way, Romeo," she said and I trudged through the yard up the two steps to my father's front porch, and knocked on the door.

"Yeah? Who is it?" my father's voice called from the other side of the door.

"It's me, Pop," I said, my voice sounding strained, even to me. It'd been a little while since I'd visited my old man, and guilt had coiled around my voice box. Now, here I was showing up unannounced, with a strange girl in tow.

"Jonah?" my father asked. I heard him rummaging around inside, followed by a rather impressive string of muffled curses. There was the sound of the deadbolt being thrown open, and then the door to my childhood home swung open.

My father isn't what most people would consider intimidating. He's around five six and checks in at around 130 pounds. Granted, it was 130 pounds of pure, stubborn tenacity and muscle that came from years of manual labor. His hair, in his younger days, had been a reddish brown, but over the years had become streaked through with silver. The same went for his beard, which could make a Viking jealous. He wore a tank top and jeans, leaving some of the tattoos that sleeved his arms and covered both sides of his chest exposed. Streaks of grease still stained his face from work.

My father looked from me, to Melly, then back to me, and sighed.

"Do you realize what time it is, boy?" he asked me, finally.

"I know, I know. I'm sorry, Pop. It's a long story."

"It usually is," he said, stepping to the side and motioning us inside. "Well, c'mon in and start talking."

The living room was simple, like pretty much everything else in the house. A couch, a worn and sagging recliner, a table beside that, and a TV on a stand in the corner. Not one of those fancy flat screens either, one of those big box types. The only picture he had hung next to his recliner. It was faded, the frame scratched. It was a picture of him and my mother, me in his lap, my sister in hers. It was taken when I was maybe four or five, which would have made my sister eleven or twelve. It had been taken before shit had gone off the rails for my family, just a month or two before my sister had killed herself, and before my mother had cut and run, to grieve or whatever it is that caused her to bail on her family. Even now that picture was harder for me to look at than I cared to admit.

"Suppose you want a cup of coffee?" my father asked me.

"That'd be great."

My father looked at me, then the kitchen, then back at me.

"I'll get right on that," I said, and wandered into the kitchen to create a little caffeinated magic.

The kitchen was the same as the living room, sparse and simple. I could hear my father talking to Melly while I made the coffee.

"I apologize for my son's lack of manners. I assure you I raised him better than that, he just has a tendency to be an ass sometimes. Benjamin Heywood, friends call me Ben."

"Melissa Trovato," I heard Melissa say. "Melly." I quirked a brow. It was strange to hear her full name.

I got two mugs out of the cabinet and poured them full of coffee, making sure to leave enough in the pot for my old man to get a refill if he so chose, lest there be hell to pay. After ensuring the sugar-to-milk ratio was correct, I spent a few minutes locked in an internal debate before ultimately deciding against adding a quick splash of something extra to my own cup of joe. Once everything was set and proper, I took both cups back into the living room. I put one on the table next to my father, who had retaken his vigil in the recliner, eyes bouncing between the two of us before he settled his eyes on Melly.

"Alright, let's hear it," he said.

I took a seat on the couch next to Melly and started nursing my coffee.

"She needs a place to stay," I said.

My father leveled me with a flat gaze.

"That right?" he asked, turning his attention back toward Melly, "I suppose it has something to do with that bruise on your cheek? Boyfriend?"

"Actually, it's not," she said.

My father took a long sip of his coffee, watching

the two of us over the rim of his cup. Neither one of us said anything.

"Well, if you want to sleep on my couch I need to know what I'm getting into. Spill. Otherwise," he said, "there's the door."

"He tried to rape me," Melly said, finally. Her voice was quiet, barely above a whisper.

There was a part of me that was angry, that much was true. There was another part of me that was disgusted that anyone would try to inflict that sort of trauma on another person. I wanted to say something, hell, say anything, but I wasn't sure what. It wasn't my place to take away from what had happened to Melly and turn it back towards me. So, I shut my mouth and let her tell the story however she needed to tell it. Out of all the ways I wanted to react, anger, disgust, some overprotective and self-serving sense of machismo, shutting up and listening felt right.

"Tell me what happened," my father said. There was something in my father's voice that made Melly relax. I'm not sure what it was, but the girl I'd picked up less than hour ago seemed to vanish. In her place was the Melly I was used to.

"I was closing the bar early. Cash came in, just before I locked up. He was stoned, all sorts of messed up. I don't know, meth maybe."

"Cash? Cash Carver? Hank's boy?" my father asked.

She nodded. I wasn't sure why, but I was a little surprised my old man knew the Carvers.

"Always was something wrong with that boy," he said.

"Right, so. He was just all over the place. Tweaking," she explained. "He followed me to the back, pushed me up against the wall. He had his hands all over me. When I tried to push him off, he punched me. I managed to grab a bottle, so I hit him hard enough to break it. He fell. He was bleeding. I ran and called Jonah. He was the first person I thought of."

"You're not overflowing with options, are you?" my father asked.

"Oh, he's not that bad," Melly said, smiling.

"He has his moments, I suppose. So you need to stay here till this Cash fellow backs off, I take it?"

"You realize I'm sitting right here, right?" I said.

They ignored me.

"I just need somewhere to stay for a few days, if that's okay?"

My father looked over at me and stared for a long second before turning his attention back to Melly.

"I suppose it should be," he said finally. "Bathroom's down the hall. You can freshen up there. I'll see if I can track down a spare blanket and a pillow for you."

My father waited until Melly was in the bathroom and he could hear water running, before he turned his attention back on me.

"So, you wanna tell me what happened to you?"

"I had a disagreement," I said.

"I'll say."

I didn't want to tell him any more. I'd borrowed the money to help him get his garage back up and running after an electrical fire had burnt up a good chunk of his tools. I never told him it was from me. Instead, I'd made one of those online funding campaigns for him and deposited the money there. As far as he knew, it was just some Good Samaritan out there in cyberspace.

"I appreciate you doing this for her, Pop," I said, setting my empty cup on the table.

"Oh, I know you do. Seems to me I got quite a bit of work around here that needs doing, we'll start there."

"I guess I owe you that much," I admitted.

"Oh, yeah, you do."

"I need to get moving, Pop. I've got some things I need to take care of."

"Uh huh," he said, sipping his coffee again.

"If she needs anything, call me?"

He didn't say anything. Instead, he stood up and trudged off down the hall and opened the linen closet. I took that as my cue and slipped out.

I needed to get home so I could start figuring out how I was going to rob one of, if not the most powerful supernatural player in the entire city.

CHAPTER 10

My trailer is a little singlewide shanty set in the back of a park filled with others single wide, rusted-out shanties. There's no underpinning, the pipes break at least six times in the winter, the roof is all but covered in rust spots, the grass is overgrown by a good six inches, and the three steps leading up to my front door are rickety and constantly threatening to fall apart. It tends to be a little too warm in the summer and not quite warm enough in the winter, but it's home. All in all, aside from the small garden of herbs I maintained in the back yard, it was pretty standard fare for the park I lived in.

I parked under the willow tree that made up the expanse of my front yard, grabbed the bottle out from under the seat, and trudged up to my door and inside. I wanted to sleep. I wanted to get something to eat. I wanted a shower.

Inside, it was a lot like outside. The carpet was threadbare and worn through in spots. The entire place smelled a little bit like cat piss from a failed experiment in pet ownership last spring. The furniture was all second-, third-, fourth-, and fifth-hand, most of it displaying upholstery patterns that would have been popular right around the same time that the girls in the porno posters decorating the Poor Confederate would have been considered *en vogue*. Like most trailers, everything was essentially connected. A small kitchen was separated from the living room by a counter top and sink. A hallway led to my bedroom, a spare room, and a bathroom.

Say what you will, I was pretty damn fond of my estate resting atop its cinderblock throne.

I poured myself a glass of water, setting the half-empty bottle on the counter top amidst a veritable army of dirty dishes and wandered towards my spare room, grabbing my old army surplus backpack from beside the couch as I went.

The spare room in my trailer was my happy place. It was bare of furnishing, save for the two levels of shelves that lined each wall and a nightstand tucked in one corner. The shelves, from start to finish, were filled with jars. Mason jars, mayo jars, those little flip top airtight jars, pretty much every type of jar was represented. Each one of them was filled with a different herb, each one grown, tended, and harvested by yours truly. Several were indigenous to other countries and had taken more than their fair share of time and care to get right. I had everything in here from condiments to lethal poisons like belladonna and night-shade. The table, covered with a thin cloth, was lined with crystals. Most of them were cheap, new-agey crap, but they too served a purpose. Crystals, stones, and the like could be used in shamanic magic to hold spirits, to create what are called "fetishes." They were one-time tricks and, for the most part, the effects only lasted a few seconds. Those few seconds, though, could be damned impressive.

I started browsing the shelves, pulling jars down and shoving them into my backpack. So far, my plan involved casing out Mama Duvalier's, once I found the place. Given her reputation, I wasn't going there with anything short of a magical arsenal, even if said arsenal was little more than a few spells and a couple of spirit fueled party favors.

I wasn't sure if it was the beatings, the crazy ladies in parking lots, or the big scary people throwing me across two lanes of black top and playing linebacker with my truck, but I damn near jumped out of my skin when I heard the knock at my door.

I stood in the center of my little war room, heart pounding against my ribs, and waited.

The knock came again.

I walked as lightly as possibly to the window, peeking out from behind the Star Wars beach towel that was proudly serving double duty as a curtain.

Sam stood outside my front door, checking his watch. After a rather massive sigh of relief that it wasn't someone else harboring the intent of doing me bodily harm, I knocked on the window, got his attention, and motioned him inside.

Sam came in, wandered his way down the hall, took a spot leaning in the doorway and watched me pluck out another two jars and add them to the bag.

"Came by to check on you," he said.

"Could be worse," I admitted.

"Could be better, too."

I grabbed another jar and put it in the bag.

"I have a feeling I'm not going to like the answer to this question, but what are you doing?" he asked.

"Inventory," I lied.

"Inventory? Looks to me like you're going to do something stupid, Jonah."

I gave Sam a quick sideways glance.

"Guilty," I admitted.

"Okay, next question. How stupid are we talking here? The I-made-a-sex-tape-with-my-best-friend's-boyfriend's-sister stupid, or are we talking the-reason-you-walk-with-a-cane stupid?"

"You're never going to let me live that down, are you?"

"Never. I'm going to remind you of it until the day you die. Now, which is it?" Sam asked.

After a minute passed and I opted to not answer, Sam made the correct conclusion.

"Right. Walking with a cane stupid it is, then."

I grabbed a few select stones from my table and added them to the bag. As if on cue, my leg shot through with a quick jolt of pain and I had to lean a little heavier on my cane. I'd met Sam five years ago, when I was eighteen and he was seventeen, living on the streets, and for all intents and purposes, eating out of trash cans. I'd stumbled across him while I was running around, pretending to be a hero. I'd had a few victories under my belt, a few wayward spirits sent back across the veil. I was arrogant, though, and we bit off more than we could chew.

One of the Fae was kidnapping girls off the street and stealing parts of their souls. Turns out, his big scheme was to use them as fuel for a spell that would erase his immortality and make him human, all so that he could commit suicide. One of those girls happened to be a friend of Sam's, one of the kids he looked out for. So, Sam and I, loaded to the gills with testosterone and bravado, walking examples of the phrase "more balls than brains," tracked him down. We'd had the intention of saving the girl. When the dust finally settled, I ended up with a shattered femur that took four surgeries and a lot of pins and screws to repair. Sam ended up with a broken jaw and a few broken ribs. We'd survived. The Fae in question didn't. Unfortunately, neither did the girl.

She died bloody.

I decided then to stop pretending I was something I wasn't: a hero. It was also around that time I started drinking. If I were one for introspective musing, I would consider it to be an important turning point in my life. Mostly, I just tried not to think about it. Ever.

"Jonah," Sam said, "What's going on?"

"It's a long story."

"Okay," Sam said, vanishing from the doorway. He came back a moment later with one of my kitchen chairs. He set it where he stood and sat, crossing his arms over his chest.

"I've got time. I just wanted to be more comfortable while you tell it to me," he said by way of explanation.

So I related everything back to him. I started with Lysone and our first meeting. Then I rehashed the incident with the Carvers, segued into another meeting with Lysone, then my trip to Abandon, and then the big scary man who put the dent in the side of my truck that my father would raise all kinds of holy hell about when he saw. I told him about Melly and Cash, then finally ended with my genius plan to assault what was, in my estimation, roughly the Death Star. When I was done, Sam was staring at me, his mouth hanging slightly open.

"Jesus," Sam said.

"I doubt he's involved."

Sam gave me a flat stare.

"Well, what can I do?" He asked.

I shrugged.

"Nothing, really."

"Bullshit."

"There's nothing you can do, Sam. I'm sort of stuck in this mess, man."

"Doesn't mean you have to fly solo," he said.

"Actually it does," I said. "This is my mess. I'm the one that has to clean it up."

"You're going to get yourself killed," Sam said, standing up. "Jesus, look at yourself. You're beat all to hell and I'm not even going to ask how much you've had to drink."

I glared at him.

"Don't look at me like that," he snapped. "I'm going with you."

"The hell you are," I said.

"Really? You're so drunk you can barely stand. What's worse, I don't even think you realize it. You spend so much time in a fucking stupor; you don't know what you're going to do when you get there. Hell, how are you going to drive there, for that matter?"

"With both hands on the wheel," I said.

"I'm serious Jonah."

"So am I," I said.

"Then like I said, I'm going with you."

I looked at Sam for a long minute. He was my best friend. Hell, he was my only friend. I had no doubt that if he came, he'd fight tooth and nail right alongside me. We'd faced scary shit together before. Hell, if it wasn't for him, I wouldn't have a "rest of my life" to be stuck using a cane for.

"Fine, but we're taking my truck."

"Done," Sam said.

"Keys are on the counter. Give me another minute?"

Sam nodded and went to get my keys. Once I had a minute of privacy, I grabbed a jar off the shelf and dumped some of the contents into my hand, then closed the jar and tossed it into my bag as well. I bit the inside of my cheek, hard enough to draw blood, and spit a small amount into the powdered herb in my palm. I gave a slight push of will, activating the inherent magical properties within the herb. The infusion of power sent a small tendril of steam rising from the dried root as the blood evaporated, fueling the magic. When Sam appeared in the doorway again, I blew the powdered herb into his face.

The Valerian burst out of my hand into a cloud, sparkling with small bits of energy. As far as magic goes, it was pretty basic stuff. Valerian root has a natural sedative property, the addition of my blood only served to intensify it, amping it up to the level of a fast-acting, pharmaceutical sleep aid. Sam coughed once and started to sway as the magic took hold. I took a few steps to catch him before he fell on the floor. As it was, all I really managed to do was catch him and send both of us into a slow topple to the carpet.

He was my best friend. I'd failed him the last time

because I wasn't good enough. All we had to show for our little adventure were some pretty gnarly scars and some even more gnarly nightmares. He'd lost someone that he'd cared deeply for.

I'd learned a lot since then. Not enough to go toe to toe with someone like Mama Duvalier, assuming the rumors were true. I just hoped that if it came to blows, I'd be able to hold my own long enough to get away. I sure as hell wasn't going to drag Sam into a mess where I could get potentially get him killed, too. That was the sort of thing I'd never come back from.

I pulled myself back up to my feet, made sure Sam was as comfortable as he could be sleeping on my floor, grabbed my bag, stopped and got the bottle off the counter, locked up behind me and started the trip to Mama Duvalier's.

CHAPTER 11

In Asheville, if you know what to look for, you can find the things that go bump in the night. Thankfully, most people don't know what to look for. Usually, it's a few scratches on a wall or a glyph of some sort hidden in some street art. Most people don't believe enough in the supernatural to start searching for their local vampire nest, witch, or pack of werewolves. The ones that did, well, silence for the bad guys is best achieved by eating the curious.

Maggie Valley was a different animal altogether. There were a few family-style tourist traps, like the Ghost Town in the Sky, but for the most part, it just wasn't populated enough to warrant any of the night (or day) time predators to take much interest in. As far as I knew, the supernatural community of Maggie Valley was pretty much Mama Duvalier.

I'd made sure to take the back roads to get here, avoiding the highways and any state troopers that might be inclined to take an interest in yours truly. Truth be told, now that I was here, I had no idea where to even start. I had a few mundane options, though I can't say any of them were very likely to yield any sort of viable results. Asking around town risked Mama Duvalier finding out that I was on the hunt for her and I wasn't exactly game on tipping my hand. I could drive around until I found something that may or may not be indicative of her presence, but that would be about as effective and timely as going door to door.

That left breaking out a little bit of the old-fashioned mojo as my only viable option. I could cross over to the spirit world, but while my soul was snooping around, it would leave me essentially comatose for however long I was on the other side. It was also my last resort, as far as I was concerned. If something happened to my spirit while it was out tripping the light fantastic on the flip side, it would be the same as dying, essentially. Sure, my body would be alive, assuming someone found it before I starved to death, but no one would be behind the wheel. I could try a spell, but any sort of casting I could do to find her would mean either exposing myself or having the spell fizzle out if she had any magical countermeasures in place, which was likely. So, I was going to have to bring in an outside consultant. A really, really outside consultant.

I had all of the necessary reagents for a summoning packed away in my bag already. Summoning a spirit is easy. Any chucklehead can summon something. It may not be the strongest spirit to ever step across the threshold between worlds, but it's doable by most folks with a little patience and a little time. Even though they're easy, it takes a bit of know and artistry to make it all go nice and smooth. It takes the right mix of herbs and a bit of blood, mixed into an ink to create the circle and sigils required to do a proper summon.

The real artistry was in painting the intended spirit's sigil. Spirits didn't have names, at least not in the way people thought of names. Some of them used names, but they didn't really own them. You can't really stand in the middle of a circle and say "Frank" over and over again, and hope that something would show up. Instead, a spirit is called with a sigil, a sort of picture writing that is unique to them and them alone. You screw up painting the sigil and the summoning could completely fizzle out. Worse, you could summon some madness-inducing tentacled horror that would find such a calling damned inconvenient and annoying.

I drove around until I found a place that I felt was fitting for the spirit that I wanted to summon. In this case, it was the dumpster behind a tourist trap seafood restaurant. It took me almost an hour to clear the pavement off, paint the circle and sigil, and prep everything for the summoning. I could have done this just about anywhere but it was a sign of respect to at least try and find a place where the spirit would be in its "natural habitat," for lack of a better term.

I took a long moment to collect my thoughts and grabbed a quick sip off the dwindling contents of my fifth, and then struck a match, tossing it onto the painted sigil. The herbs in the ink, mixed with my blood, flared up almost waist high as the magic contained in them was released in a sudden torrent. When they finally died down, a rat spirit sat in the center of the circle, directly on top of the sigil. It looked, for the most part, like a normal gray furred rat. Well, a normal rat that just so happened to be roughly the size of a Doberman Pinscher. It stared at me, head tilted almost comically to the side. Its right ear, which was every bit as large as my palm, was scarred and tattered, the physical memory of a scrap from days long past. Its tail, roughly as long as my arm and as thick as my wrist at the base, was a grayish pink that reminded me of corpse flesh. Perfect, ink-like black eyes examined my face with a level of intelligence that went far above and beyond what you see in most people, let alone rodents.

"Moki," I said flatly, by way of greeting.

Gretchen had worked with Moki for years. When I was a kid, he was the spirit that used to watch over me when she couldn't. He'd served as a guardian for me in the spirit world, protecting me from things I never even saw. That said, he wasn't really what I'd call a friend. Actually, I was pretty sure he still considered me more of a pain in the ass than anything.

"Boy, you look like about ten pounds of crap in a five-pound bag," Moki said, his voice accentuated by a long southern drawl.

Yep, he could talk. At great length if given the opportunity.

"Wow," I said. "You're a peach."

The rat spirit's ear twitched.

"I need your help," I said, after a moment of silently staring at each other.

"What else is new?" he sighed.

"I'm serious," I said.

"Me too. What do you want, Jonah?"

"I need your help. I told you that."

"Obviously. The hell you want?"

"I'm looking for something."

Moki stared at me for a moment and I suddenly felt like that kid who got called up to the blackboard in Math class and had absolutely no idea what the answer to the problem was.

"Well?"

"I'm looking for a piece of a runestone."

"You called me here for a rock?"

"Not exactly."

"Well get to the point, then."

"I need to know where I can find Mama Duvalier."

Moki looked surprised.

"The hell are you looking for her for?"

"Nothing good," I said.

"Obviously. You messing with that lot, you've done and moved up into the big leagues, kid, and as much as I hate to say it, you ain't ready to play on that level," Moki said.

"Yeah. I get that. Can you tell me where to find her or not?"

"Chances are, she already knows you're nosing around. She's smart like that and you ain't exactly what any would call subtle. But to answer your question, yeah, I could tell you where to find her."

"Alright, where?"

"I said could, not would. First things first. What's in it for me?"

That's the problem with spirits. Nothing, absolutely nothing, with them is free. There's always a price. It's usually a lot less expensive than what you'd pay one of the Fae for a favor, but there's always a price nonetheless. Usually, it involves paying some form of tribute to their earthly counterparts.

Spirits are essentially thoughtforms, mankind's collective impression of something given form. For instance, a wolf here is just a wolf. A wolf in the spirit world is about eight feet tall at the shoulders, with glowing red eyes, an insatiable hunger, and a really bad attitude. Not because that's what a wolf is at its core, but because over time that's what mankind has envisioned them as. It's the image they've created. That much belief gives something form. You start adding religion into the mix, and things can get pretty hinky.

"What do you want? The usual?" I asked.

"I want you to go home, get drunk, well, drunker and forget this nonsense."

"I can't do that."

"And why the hell the not?"

I explained the whole story, from Lysone on down the list. Moki didn't say a word, he just listened, tilting his head this way and that as I recounted the events.

"I s'pose that's as good a reason as any," Moki said.

"Yeah," I said. "So? Tell me?"

"After we discuss terms," Moki said.

I sighed.

"Alright, what do you want?"

"Assuming you survive this little suicide mission, order some wrestling on Pay Per View."

"What?"

"You heard me."

"You're serious," I said.

"As a heart attack."

"You're not a physical being," I said.

"Yeah, and? Summon me."

I shook my head, irritated.

"Sure, fine. Okay. It's a deal. If I survive, you get your burly man in spandex fix."

"Farm, little ways off Tater Patch Road. Look for the bottle trees. Follow that up a few miles, then hit the dirt road off the side. It'll take you up a ways."

"Tater Patch Road? Seriously?"

"You are in the South, Jonah."

"Wow," I said. "That's, just…wow."

"Can I go now? I ain't in the mood to watch you run off and do something stupid."

I nodded and reached out with the tip of my shoe, smudging the circle. Moki started to fade away, slowly becoming transparent before finally vanishing. I stood there for a few minutes after he was gone, listening to the slow buzz of the occasional car on the road behind me. I turned, almost tripped on an empty beer bottle and in a moment of frustration kicked it towards the dumpster, missed, and watched it shatter on the pavement.

I'd be lying if I said it didn't feel a little prophetic.

CHAPTER 12

I didn't have to drive long to find the bottle trees that Moki had told me about. Bottle trees are a common occurrence in the South, most often connected to hoodoo. The general belief is that the blue bottles catch spirits, trapping them until the sun rises. Mama Duvalier's property was lined with them, one bottle tree every hundred or so feet, each one standing out in stark contrast to the thick woods behind them.

I made a few passes up and down the street before I finally worked up the nerve to pull my truck off the road. I found a spot about a quarter mile away from where the road diverged from the paved street and made the transition to dirt. I waited for almost fifteen minutes, and after no other cars passed, I got out and started to hoof it towards Mama Duvalier's. A steady rain was falling, which, despite soaking me to the bone (again) and making my leg ache like hell (again), was a benefit. The rain offered me a little bit of cover in the sense that it'd be hard as hell to hear me picking my way through the woods and would, I was hoping, drive anyone inside that could potentially see me on my approach.

I made it maybe three steps over the property line when I heard the first bottle break. More started bursting in rapid succession, filling the air with loud, gunshot-like pops and the high-pitched chatter of glass against glass.

By the time I managed to put two and two together, I was already in it up to my eyeballs. The bottle trees weren't made for capturing spirits, at least these weren't. Every one of the bottles was a fetish, holding a rather restless spirit hostage. I'll give credit where credit is due, as far as home alarm systems went, this one was, for lack of a better term, effective.

Wind spirits, dozens of them, came tearing through the trees, each one howling mad and fixated on me. Pine needles, leaves, and pieces of debris, along with the rain, kicked up into my face and eyes in their wake. A burst of wind, gale force at the least, hit me in the side. That, along with the slippery terrain and the fact that I was mostly relying on my cane for balance, sent me into a sideways tumble that ended with me landing in a thicket of briars. Thorns, more annoyance than pain, tore at my hands and cheeks. It took a minute for me to get untangled, but when I managed to get to my knees, another blast of wind hit me in the gut, like a massive fist, hard enough to launch me several feet into the air and then back to the ground.

I hit hard. Harder than I would've expected, given that I was landing on mud-soaked ground. For a moment, the world swam in front of my eyes, colors from the spirit world bleeding over into my field of vision, turning everything into a crazy, mixed-up kaleidoscope of warring realities. I realized I'd pretty much just walked right into Mama Duvalier's hands just as I lost consciousness.

• • •

I've had this dream more times than I could count. Every time, it opened the same old wound. It brought to life a hurt so deep and profound that the echo of it carried over into wakefulness and had a tendency to follow me around like some kind of phantom passenger.

There was something different this time, though, something that wasn't familiar. It was still the house I'd spent the first part of my life in, the little three-bedroom home in Portland, Oregon. Only it didn't look lived in, or at least not lived in recently. The furniture was still there, but it was old, waterlogged, heavy with mold. The windows were covered in filth, turning the world outside into little more than a hazed-over blur. I knew this place well enough to find my way through it in the dark. My room was on the right side of the hall. My sister's directly across. The bathroom, where I'd sit on the edge of the bathtub while she got ready for school, was next to her room. My parents' room was at the end of the hall. The living room and kitchen were connected with an open doorway, laced over with cobwebs. The storm was still there, whipping the trees back and forth outside, lightning painting the night sky in flashes of blue and white. I could smell the bacon from breakfast that morning mixing with the warm, almost sugary, smell of my father's pipe tobacco.

It was here too. The thing that took my sister away from

me. I could feel it. I could almost taste it, just underneath the comforting smells of home, like rotting, fetid meat and stagnant water.

The woman from the parking lot of the Poor Confederate was standing in the kitchen. For a long moment, I stared at her, trying to wrap my brain around her presence. I'd had this dream hundreds, if not thousands of times, and it never changed. Yet here she was, larger than life and twice as ugly.

"You're not supposed to be here," I said.

She shrugged. She was wearing the same tattered jeans, but she'd replaced the Mötley Crüe shirt with a Skid Row shirt. Her hair hung around her face in matted tangles, which didn't help to make her look any more sane than she had the first time I came across her.

"I'm not supposed to be anywhere," she said, matter of fact. Something caught her attention that I couldn't hear despite my familiarity with this nightmare landscape and she turned towards the back of the house. She stood there staring out the window over the kitchen sink. She flickered, briefly, like a bad film reel, and then vanished.

I opened my mouth to say something, though I'm not entirely sure what it was I was actually planning on saying.

The crazy things about dreams is that even when you know what's going to happen, sometimes, no matter how good you are at controlling it, you can't change the outcome.

Thunder came next, booming from everywhere all at once, a sonic assault so loud that, in my dream, the dust lifted off of shelves, dishes rattled against each other in the cupboards, and cracks started to thread their way through the drywall.

What came next was the part that hurt the most.

My sister screamed, a banshee-like wail that carried out over the sound of the thunder. It was the pure and utter terror and pain of it that always got me. Her screaming, with the storm raging outside, when everything should have been peaceful and still, that was something that I just could never shake, even now.

I tried running to her room, as I always did every time this scenario played itself out. I found myself moving in that slow motion that's commonplace in dreams, like my legs had been encased in lead.

It took something like an ice age before I reached her room. I had expected to see my sister sitting up in her bed, her dark hair mussed from sleep. That's how it happened before. I'd run into her room, she'd stare at me, I'd see that thing in her eyes, she'd bleed from the gunshot wound she'd inflict on herself, and I'd wake up.

It was different this time.

My sister was sitting on her bed; that much was the same. She was smiling. A shadow slithered across the floor, sliding over the wall and towards her bed. Everything about its shape, the way it moved, the curves and angles that comprised its form, were all nausea inducing. It was Lovecraftian, a thing that didn't belong in this world. The shadows coalesced into a vaguely humanoid shape, and for a moment, there was a face present, though only in the most rudimentary of ways. It turned towards me, locking its eyes with mine as it materialized into a solid, human-like form next to my sister, and smiled.

I tried to scream, to charge towards what, at the time I thought was a monster, but I couldn't move. My legs, my voice, every part of my body was on lockdown, the signals from my brain refusing to reach out to the parts I needed to work. I learned later what it was that took my sister. A manifestation of millions of people's faith in something wholly evil. It was a walking, talking, if not wholly physical, incarnation of one of the seven deadly sins.

A demon.

It watched me, even though it had no eyes. Instead there were just two spots where there weren't shadows inside the facsimile of a face. After a few seconds of staring at me, one of those empty spots filled with darkness.

It took me a second to realize what it was doing, but once I had, my fear only intensified.

It winked at me.

The shadows swirled around my sister, enveloping her. She shot back on the bed, her body going rigid. I tried to run towards her, to help, but I couldn't move. She started to convulse, her tiny body thrashing back and forth, slamming against the mattress.

When she finally went still, the storm outside had stopped. I could hear her breathing, slow, measured and steady. She sat up, locking her eyes with mine, and spoke in a voice that wasn't even remotely human.

"Remember me."

CHAPTER 13

I woke up with a sudden jerk. It took me a minute to sort through the myriad of visuals that came with waking up and put up the necessary mental walls so that I wasn't overwhelmed. The echoes of the dream were still rattling around in my skull and the copper taste of adrenaline and fear was still heavy on my tongue. I hurt all over, which I didn't consider too much of a surprise, but my face was really singing. My hands were behind my back and I could feel the bite of something against my wrists. Zip ties, maybe. I checked my ankles and found them bound as well with, as suspected, zip ties.

It took a bit of wriggling around, but I managed to sit up and take stock of my surroundings. I was in a root cellar. The floor under me was raw earth. The walls on three sides were lined in shelves, all filled to the brim with canned vegetables. My cane was a few feet away, leaning against a rickety wooden set of stairs. My backpack, unfortunately, was nowhere to be found. The floor overhead was old wooden planks, thin slivers of light shining through the cracks between the boards. I could hear conversation, but I was only able to make out every couple of words, not enough to piece together what was being said. Every so often, someone would walk by overhead, casting shadows down into the basement.

Not that it would have mattered, really. I was tied up in the basement of Appalachia's resident wicked witch and I wasn't exactly feeling like this was going to play out in my favor. Anything I heard wasn't really going to do me a whole lot of good. My best bet was to focus on what was important: getting the hell out of here.

I was still trying to figure out exactly how I was going to try and get out of here, when the door at the top of the stairs opened. The light was brighter than I expected, and for a second, all I could see were shadowed forms as a small parade made its way into the basement. When my eyes adjusted to the new light source, I was surrounded by a semicircle of women. Under different circumstances I probably wouldn't have been bothered to find myself in such a predicament.

The women all bore similar sharp, angular features. Sisters, maybe, or possibly cousins. They all looked to be roughly within a few years of each other, age wise. They had the same mocha-colored skin, the same dark hair, each one styled differently.

"Hi?" I said, finally.

They didn't say anything.

"Okay?" I said. "How does this work exactly? I've never been held hostage."

Still nothing.

It wasn't until Mama Duvalier came down the steps a moment later, that some sort of reaction passed between them. It was a mixture of hushed respect and military-like discipline. Postures straightened, heads lowered just a bit, and an air of all around respect filled the little root cellar.

Mama Duvalier shared the same features as my three captors. On the women, the high cheekbones and sharp chins looked severe. On Mama Duvalier they looked almost regal, cut with a haughty arrogance. She carried herself with the swagger that came with authority, of orders and commands carried out within seconds, with no argument, and hell befall anyone that chose otherwise.

Mama Duvalier was on the heavy side, though it was the sort of broad-shouldered build that spoke to muscle, not fat. Her hair was cut short, tight to the scalp, and peppered here and there with bits of silver. She wore jeans, hiking boots, and a light-blue flannel shirt. Everything about her read hard work, grit, and pit bull–like tenacity, from the clothes to the way she moved.

One of the girls standing around me moved to across the cellar and grabbed a chair from under the stairs. She carried it over and set it in front of me, then returned to her previous position of looming over me.

Mama Duvalier sat down across from me and leveled me with a stare that made me feel like I was two inches tall and in my underwear, all at once.

"So, you're him," she said, leaning back and throwing an arm over the back of the chair. It was frighteningly casual, like I wasn't even close to being taken seriously, let alone considered a threat. Her voice was a lot warmer than

I expected. It was kind, patient sounding, with just a touch of a French accent.

"I guess that depends on who the him in question is?"

"C'mon now. You're Gretchen's little apprentice and you're all grown up. I must say, you grew up pretty, Jonah."

The hell? Was she flirting with me? For once, I didn't know what to say.

"I heard she passed. You have my condolences."

"Thanks," I mumbled, mostly unsure of how to respond. I'd been expecting a lot of things from the evil queen of the Appalachians, but I was pretty sure this level of civility wasn't one of them. She wasn't exactly being kind, as evidenced by the fact that I was zip tied in her basement, but she wasn't being out and out hostile. At least, not yet.

"Though, I can't say she'd be too proud of you," she said, looking over me one more time. "Given you've turned into a pretty piss poor rendition of her example."

And, nevermind.

"Yeah? I try to set the bar low," I said. "Keeps people from expecting too much out of me."

"No need to be wiseass," Mama Duvalier said, her tone doing more to dissuade me than the goon squad and the bindings put together. "Facts is facts, you're an alcoholic who cons good, hard-working people out of their money. I ain't condemning you for it, but I sure don't abide by it either. Actually, it's a bit of a shame really."

"Yeah, and why's that?"

"Because you've been doing nothing but drowning any potential you might have underneath a whole lot of booze and even more self-loathing."

"You don't know the first thing about me," I said.

"Don't I?" Mama Duvalier asked. She undid the top button on her shirt and reached into it, withdrawing a battered pack of cigarettes and a lighter. She tapped one out, lit it, and replaced the pack. She watched me for a long time, taking the occasional drag from her coffin nail and letting the smoke spiral into a haze that hung just over her head. "I know more than you think. I know why you walk with that cane, for one. I know why you drink. It ain't because some girl went and got herself dead, either. At least, not the one you convince yourself it is. Honest, I know more about you than you know about yourself, Mister Jonah. More important, I know that how you go through the next few days, it's gonna set the tone of things for a long time."

"You say that like you're going to let me walk out of here," I said.

She looked a little surprised.

"Why wouldn't you?"

"Well, zip tying me and throwing me in your basement doesn't exactly bode too well for me."

"You came onto my property with a small arsenal."

I hadn't even thought about that. I had just walked up to her front door with the magical equivalent of a loaded gun. Several loaded guns, actually. Maybe even a hand grenade or two. It wasn't entirely unreasonable that she would take that as an insult.

"I knew you'd show up on my doorstep one day," she said. "Granted, I had hoped it would be under different circumstances."

"So what, are we supposed to be friends?"

"Well, that depends."

"On?"

"Well, I'll put it to you like this: it's up to you. I am willing to let you walk out of here safe and sound. Call it respect for your dearly departed teacher. Though, there's a condition."

"Yeah?"

"That thing you're looking for, stop."

"I'm sorry?"

"That runestone. You need to stop looking for it."

"Trust me, I want to."

She narrowed her eyes at me, surveying my face.

"You want to, but you can't."

"I can't," I agreed.

"That's a shame, Jonah, and damned disappointing. You're willing to trade your life for a little bit of money. Gretchen's rolling over in her grave," she said, a slight hint of disgusting in her tone.

"It's not about the money," I said.

"Maybe so," Mama Duvalier said, standing slowly, moving with the sort of calculated caution that came with old age and aching joints. "You sure this is the way you want this to go, Jonah?"

I sat there, staring at the floor. I wasn't stupid. I knew which way it was going to play out, but I didn't want to think about it. I didn't want to die, but my old man had sacrificed most of his life trying to make mine better. He'd spent countless amounts of money and hours putting me before himself and gained only frustration, heartache, and pain. The Carvers wouldn't make it clean, either, if they hurt him because I didn't pay them. They'd make the old man suffer and I couldn't abide that.

"Positive," I said finally, and took a long, slow breath.

I wasn't necessarily resigned to my fate, but I wasn't exactly in a position to fight my way out.

"Maryse, dear?"

"Yes, Momma?"

"You know what to do, baby. Make it easy on him. Give him that much, alright?"

"Yes, Momma," the woman in the middle said. She was taller than the other two, thinner, and wore her hair in shoulder-length dreadlocks adorned with shells and beads. She walked casually to one of the shelves and lifted a long, thin bladed kitchen knife from somewhere amidst the various canning jars.

The other two women grabbed me, pushing me down onto the floor and pinning me there. I struggled, maybe not as resigned to my fate as I'd fooled myself into thinking. Mama Duvalier's daughters were deceptively strong, lifting my arms up over my head and stretching me out, making sure that Maryse had easy access to all of my squishy bits.

She knelt down beside me and put the blade against my side, the tip just between my ribs, right beside my heart.

And just like that, the lights went out.

CHAPTER 14

A certain measure of confusion comes with being plunged into sudden darkness. When the lights go out at home, say during a big storm, you sit there, staring around with a dumb expression on your mug until your brain processes a very simple idea: the lights are out.

For the span of several heartbeats, none of us moved. Hell, we barely even breathed. There was a building tension in the air, something tangible and electric enough that it put my teeth on edge.

"Momma?" one of the three women asked, her voice pitched to a low whisper.

A response came in the form of a heavy thump against the floor overhead. Whatever it was, it was big and hit hard enough to send small clouds of dust raining down onto us. I didn't take that as a good sign.

"That doesn't sound good, at all," I said.

"Shush, boy," Mama Duvalier said.

"What do we do, Momma?" another one of her

daughters asked. She didn't sound overly concerned about whatever it was that was going on. If anything, she sounded impatient.

Mama Duvalier didn't speak, letting another stretch of silence fill the basement.

Of course, it was just a precursor to that moment when all hell breaks loose.

The door to the basement exploded inwards in a burst of splinters and noise. A body—a very large, unconscious body—came tumbling down the stairs. The slab of humanity came to a stop at the base of the stairs and lay there, perfectly still.

Mama Duvalier and her brood forgot about me for the moment, focusing on the commotion upstairs. Light was flooding into the basement now, almost blinding in the aftermath of the recent darkness.

"Maryse, Gabrielle, go!" Mama Duvalier snapped, then turned her attention back to me. The woman who'd only moments ago been ready to plunge a knife into me and the other girl, Gabrielle, bolted up the stairs. Thankfully, they took the knife with them.

Duvalier turned towards me, her eyes alit with a horrifying, absolutely blood-curdling, rage. She reached out, grabbing me by the hair, and jerked me to my feet.

"You bring them with you?" she snarled.

"What? No," I stammered.

She was about to say something, but was cut off by the sounds of utter calamity upstairs. I could hear furniture breaking, the sound of a fight, glass shattering, and a scream of pain.

It was one of her kids.

"Watch him," she snapped to the last woman in the basement.

Mama Duvalier stormed up the stairs, and I had the strangest feeling that whoever had made the mistake of attacking her home was about to find themselves FUBARed in short order. The girl she'd left in the basement to stand guard looked from me to the stairs, indecision warring on her face. I got it, a part of her wanted to go, to rush upstairs and help her family. Hell, it's what got me into this mess to begin with.

She looked to be around the same age as me, if not younger. Compared to her mother and her sisters, she had a much slighter build, though she easily had a few inches over her other family members in the height department. Overhead, the sounds of the fight were getting a bit more distant, like the combat had moved outside.

"Don't suppose you'd just untie me, would you?"

"Shush," she said, her eyes darting between me and the open doorway at the top of the stairs.

"Yeah, didn't think so," I said.

Something about this whole attack didn't make a whole lot of sense to me. Why would they not come down here? We were all sitting ducks; the only way out was up the stairs. Hell, they didn't even need to come down here to do us all in. They could've just as easily stood at the top of the stairs and sprayed gunfire downward, or thrown a make-shift bomb, or blocked off the door and burnt the place down around us. Instead, they'd lured Mama Duvalier and her daughters out of the basement, leaving me down here with, well, that was another damn good question, wasn't it?

"So, Warden, if you're gonna be babysitting me, what do I call you?" I asked.

The girl turned her eyes towards me with annoyance.

"Right, shut up. I know."

"Mia," she said, then turned her eyes back towards the door at the top of the stairs, or lack thereof.

"Mia, huh?" I said, trying to figure out if there was a way I could talk my way out of this after all. Mama Duvalier and her other sisters weren't here at the moment and Mia didn't look like she was exactly overflowing with confidence, either. Both things I could maybe spin to my favor. At the very least, I may be able to buy some more time or pick up a small tidbit of information on the off chance that I did manage to get out of here with my skin intact.

Mia started pacing back and forth across the basement, glancing towards the door every few seconds, everything about her humming with nervous energy.

Something hit the side of the house, loud enough to rattle the place on its foundations. A few of the jars fell from the shelves, filling the basement with the acrid smell of vinegar.

That was all it took and Mia forgot about me, bolting up the stairs to aid her family.

Which suited me just fine. Once she'd cleared the stairs and vanished, I squirmed over to the broken jars. It took me a minute to find a piece of glass large enough to cut the bindings around my wrists, and another minute to cut the ones at my ankles.

Once I'd managed to get myself free, I worked my way up to vertical. My hands and feet were alight with pins and needles, and coupled with my bum leg made it almost impossible to stand. I used the shelving to brace myself. My face stung where the Carvers had cut me, but all in all the pain was mostly manageable.

I grabbed my cane and started working my way up the steps, pausing every few seconds to try and gauge the conflict on sound alone. I wasn't sure what was going on outside, but whatever it was, it had gone from muted thuds and bangs, to loud and violent. In the last few seconds, someone had turned the intensity way up. The air was practically humming with magic. There were powers flying around outside that I didn't really understand or have any familiarity with, but they were frighteningly strong nonetheless.

The stairway led up to a hallway, which led into a kitchen at one end and what I assumed was the front door at the other. There were a few more doorways along the wall heading towards the kitchen, all of them closed. After waiting a minute to make sure nothing was going to take my head off, I stepped out into the hallway.

I'd expected a lot more for someone with Mama Duvalier's reputation. A little more opulence, maybe, or a little more terror. Maybe some pentacles drawn in blood or something. Instead, there was just a lot of cheap furniture and ugly, floral print wallpaper. Oh, and chickens. Lots of chickens. Statues, pictures, curtains, the works. I would have preferred the bloody pentacles.

For a minute, I considered the front door and if I'd known what I was walking into, I probably would've taken it. As it was, I didn't think I'd be able to do much against whatever it was on the other side with just my cane.

Instead, I kept close to the wall and drifted towards

the kitchen, trying doors as I went. The first opened onto a bedroom. Same for the second.

The third, however, was secured with a padlock. As a general rule, people only lock up things they either don't want other people to take or don't want other people to see. A slave to my very curious (and dare I say charming) nature, I really, really wanted to see what was behind that door.

Thankfully, I had a way with locks. They'd been an obsession of mine when I was a kid, and no doubt that obsession had led a lot of the doctors towards diagnosing me with autism. Up until I'd met Gretchen, I used locks as a way to block out all the weird things I was seeing on a regular basis as a kid. I could recite specs on probably half a dozen different company lines from rote memory and learned to pick most of them in about three seconds, give or take. As a general rule, I kept a lock pick in the lining of my jacket, just in case. It took me a second to wiggle it out, but once I did, I had the lock opened in record time.

I slipped inside and came face to face with what made Mama Duvalier who she is.

The entire room was one big voodoo altar, complete with candles, cigars, bottles of booze, blood, chalk drawings on the floor and walls, skulls, feathers, the works. Beside the massive altar, the only other things in the room were a few waist-high stacks of books. Even those were serving as makeshift tables for spell components or ritual gear.

Mama Duvalier was a Mambo, a voodoo priestess. It explained a lot about the rumors attributed to her. Everything I'd heard about her, the potions, the magic, the cursing of jilted lovers, all fell under that purview.

Voodoo was another one of those things that the

movies got all wrong. In movies, voodoo is all about curses and voodoo dolls, that sort of thing. A true Mambo, or Houngan, was touched by the divine. They were, essentially, descended from the Loa, the very spirits they channeled. It was those spirits that let them do the curses and create the voodoo dolls that voodoo practitioners were famous for, but it also let them control the weather, get the dead up and moving around, and all sorts of other nastiness. There were maybe twenty real-deal, full-fledged voodoo practitioners in the world, at least that I knew of. Most of them lived in the traditional locales, West Africa, Haiti, one or two in New Orleans. All of them had one thing in common though: they could summon down beings every bit as strong as angels or demons, and channel that power. They were, for all intents and purposes, the children of gods.

I gave the room a quick once over, saw my bag sitting next to the door, scooped it up and gave it a check to make sure all of my stuff was still there. Satisfied, I grabbed a bottle of what looked like rum from off the altar (which was probably some kind of sacrilege), and a couple of the books, shoved them all into my bag and threw it over my shoulder. I was ready to wrap up my little act of spiteful petty larceny, when something caught my eye.

Tucked in behind the altar was a small bundle wrapped in what looked like hides or leather and covered in an occult script. If I hadn't stopped to give the room one last look, I'd have missed it completely. I have no idea how, or why, but once I saw it, I knew instantly what it was.

The stone.

I crossed the room and grabbed the stone off the floor. As soon as I put my hand on it, I could feel pure energy radiating off it, even through the leather and hide bindings. Though, energy was probably the wrong word to describe what I felt when I picked it up. It was potential—the potential of power, of possibilities, and none of them were good. It was like holding a bomb in the palm of your hand. The potential was there, all the faith in the old stories, in the depictions that had been carved into the larger rune stone, that mystical energy, just waiting to be unleashed.

I shoved the rock into my bag, along with everything else and tossed it back over my shoulder. Outside, I could hear the sounds of the fighting, along with the all too close rumble of thunder. I still had no idea who was throwing down with Mama Duvalier. From the sound of it, whoever it was they were giving her one hell of a run for her money.

I slipped back into the hallway, tried to ignore the splashes of red on the hardwood floor, and made my way towards the kitchen, and thankfully, the back door.

I pulled the door open, stepped in front of a small, screen-enclosed back door and stopped dead in my tracks. I wanted absolutely nothing more than to get the hell out of dodge. It's just hard to move when you get a blatant reminder of just how insignificant and vulnerable you are in the face of real power.

CHAPTER 15

The rain was pouring in a violent, nearly blinding sheet of water. I could make out a few figures through the haze, standing on the wide expanse of open grass that made up Mama Duvalier's backyard. I could see just enough to spot Mama Duvalier and her brood amidst the torrent. All things considered, they were holding their own. That wasn't what freaked me out when I had stepped out of the house. It was Mama Duvalier's shadow: she shouldn't have had one. And if she did, it wouldn't look like this.

The shadow stretched out behind her for at least ten feet. It was thinner than Mama Duvalier, the limbs a little too long, the shape of the clothing different. I could make out tuxedo tails and a top hat, and yet its movements matched hers perfectly.

Their opponents flickered through the rain, seemingly disappearing from one place and reappearing at another. Mama Duvalier made a few simple motions with one hand, her daughters would gesture in their opponents' general direction, and three or four at a time would just disintegrate.

I'd never seen magic or power like that get thrown around so easily. Sure, I'd seen a few big workings here and there, but this was a whole other level.

It was also my cue to get to stepping.

I hit the woods at what approximates to a run for a guy with one fully functional leg. I didn't even really know if I was going in the right direction. Though, to be fair, I considered anything away from the chaos behind me to be close enough to right that I was willing to take my chances. My mind screamed a million different things at me as I stumbled blindly through the trees, surrounded by the roar of the rain. I couldn't help but feel elated, having gotten the prize that I'd come for from someone who, by all accounts, was terrifying. Given what I'd seen and experienced in my short foray into Casa de Duvalier, I had little reason to doubt the rumors, even if it was a little easier than I'd expected. More than that, I'd gotten out alive and, all things considered, not too much worse for the wear. Then there was fear, fear for my life, fear of what I'd discovered about the old granny witch that I'd heard so much about. Fear of what she'd do when she discovered the fact that I'd just ripped her off.

That, however, was a problem for another day.

I ran for what I thought was maybe ten minutes, though with all the madness going on behind me, it could've been a less than a minute or as long as half an hour. Everything had turned into a massive, adrenaline-fueled blur. In my flight, it all turned into trees, rain, noise, and flashes of lightning. Truth be told, it was probably the adrenaline, but there was a certain lightness in my step that if I weren't in danger of imminent death or dismemberment, I might've enjoyed. As it was, I was far enough into the woods that the sounds of the fight had faded out to a distant echo, drowned out by the roar of the rain.

I saw my truck, outlined against the darkening sky, barely visible through the trees. A surge of relief and fresh adrenaline washed over me, sending me crashing through the underbrush. I pushed harder, covering as much ground as I could with each hobbled, half-there step.

I was maybe ten yards away from my truck when I felt a familiar wave of power wash over me, strong enough to stop me mid-stride. A second later, the girl from the parking lot of the Poor Confederate stepped out from behind a small copse of trees, putting herself between myself and salvation.

"You have the stone," she said, more a statement than question. Even though her voice was barely a whisper, I could hear it with crystal clarity over the din of the rain.

"You know what you have to do now, right?"

"Yeah, it's pretty apparent. Keep running," I said, taking a step to the side. She sidestepped, still a good ten feet away from me and put herself once more between my truck and myself. The message was clear. I was going to hear what she had to say, my opinion on the matter be damned.

"You have to make sure this plays out to its end. Its proper end," she said.

"Look, this is enlightening and all, but I really need to continue running for my life. So if you don't mind?"

She pointed to the woods behind me.

I really don't know why I did it. I don't know why I didn't just get my ass back in gear, but I looked over my shoulder in the direction she was pointing.

One of Mama Duvalier's daughters, Maryse I think her name was, had spotted me, and was currently making a beeline through the trees in my direction. Her clothes were soaked, plastered to her skin. She was all but painted in what I could only assume was blood. The rain had streaked through the gore on her cheeks and forehead, giving her a nearly animalistic countenance.

"It's going to get worse. They're going to think you did this."

"Did what?"

The girl, whoever she was, held up a hand, palm out. The feeling of power that radiated off of her, in that instance, was freakishly intense. It was like standing next to a lightning strike. There was a brief instant of tension filling the air. Then it was gone. At the same instant that the girl unleashed the power she'd gathered around her hand, Maryse's head whipped to the side with an audible crack. It sounded like someone stepping on a dry branch. For a moment, Maryse stood where she was, wavering on her feet. Her eyes were wide, her mouth slightly open, like she was surprised, or shocked, and the emotion hadn't quite gathered up enough steam to pass her lips and turn into a vocalization. She fell into a crumpled heap, her head at a wholly unnatural angle.

I tried to say something. Instead, I stammered over a few random syllables, that maybe on a good day, could be pieced into some approximation of "what the hell."

I turned back to look at the girl from the Poor Confederate, but she was gone.

I bolted towards my truck. I climbed inside the cab, got the engine running, put a good mile and a half between me and Mama Duvalier's little compound, and made no effort to rationalize what had just happened.

I fishtailed into the first reasonably full parking lot I could find, which just so happened to belong to a Walmart. Under normal circumstances, I considered Walmart's to be the physical equivalent of the third level of Dante's hell.

This time, though, I just found it strangely comforting. It didn't make the fear go away, it changed it. There was something about being around people, about being somewhere mundane, away from voodoo priestesses and imminent death that at least turned the icy fear into a familiar, bone-deep, chill.

It didn't help that the mystery girl, the one who'd snapped Maryse's neck, had said that the Duvalier family would blame me for her death. Despite the fact that it was highly plausible that Maryse had died in the chaos of the attack on Mama Duvalier's, it wasn't outside the realm of possibility that the Voodoo Priestess of Appalachia would believe I had murdered one of her daughters.

I sat there for a long time, watching the rain trace odd, asymmetrical patterns on the windshield and strange liquid shadows across the dashboard and seat.

I reached over and grabbed my backpack out of the floorboard, setting it on the seat beside me. I opened it, dumping the contents on the passenger seat. Most of my gear was still there, the fetishes, the herbs, and so on and so forth. The books and the bottle I'd taken were there, as was the hide-wrapped bundle.

I grabbed the bottle, opened it, and took a long pull. The rum was unlike anything I'd ever tasted. It was spicy, sort of sweet, and potent. Almost instantly my nerves started to settle, some of the shake slid out of my hands, and my head started to clear.

I picked up the first book, a thick, cloth-bound textbook, and started flipping through the pages. It was in French, I think. Either way, I couldn't make heads or tails of it. Latin, some of the other dead languages, weren't really a problem for me, given that most magic treatises and texts were written in dead languages. I was all but fluent in Avalonian, the language of the Fae. I could even wing a little Infernal in a pinch. Languages still used by large swaths of the world were the ones I just couldn't wrap my head around. Go figure. Languages spoken by face-eating monsters, not a problem. Languages spoken by actual living people, and I was clueless. At the very least, I could probably make a few bucks off of it.

The other book was smaller, maybe four inches wide by ten inches tall. This one I recognized as soon as I saw the first page. That's not to say I knew what it was per se, but I knew what it was all about. The circles, the occult symbols, the mixture of runic languages, I knew enough to know that I was holding some major mojo. This was a summoning book. Judging from the bits and pieces I could make out, it had the metaphorical names, addresses, and phone numbers of some pretty big, pretty nasty stuff. I flipped a few more pages and shoved it back in my bag. That one it was best to leave alone.

I took a few more minutes to collect my nerves. When I finally felt like I was capable of keeping my head on straight, I pulled out of the parking spot and started trucking my way back towards Asheville.

CHAPTER 16

By the time I got to my father's neighborhood, the storm had let up and the setting sun was playing off of the rest of the rain clouds in a staggeringly beautiful mix of purples and reds.

As I drove through the last few side streets that led to my old man's house, I could see more lights coming on, families settling into dinners and relaxing after a hard day at work. There was a whole sense of suburban peace about it that got to me. Maybe it was the way my family had gone, after my sister's suicide, that really made it sting. Once she'd died and my mother had left, it was just me and my pop. That's not taking anything away from the old guy, but his time was spent working nonstop to make ends meet, and any free time he had was spent sitting in front of doctors, specialists, or the occasional quack. I started longing for something sort of normal. At least, I did in retrospect.

I pulled over to the curb across the street from my old man's house and climbed out of the truck, leaving my backpack on the floorboard. I was still soaking wet. My little exodus through the woods had left a deep, steady ache in my leg, which left me leaning on my cane a lot heavier than I would've liked. The lights in my father's house were out, and his truck was gone, which wasn't surprising. He had a tendency to work late, more often than not. Given everything Melly had been through, it wouldn't surprise me in the slightest if she were still asleep.

I made my way up the little walk and to the front door and stopped.

Something wasn't right. I stood on the porch, wrestling with a bout of indecision. After a few minutes of uneventful silence, I just chalked it up to a case of lingering nerves.

The living room was empty, with just enough of the fading daylight filtering in to cast the room in heavy shadows.

"Melly?"

I waited for a second, and when there was no response, I stepped further into the house.

"Melly, you here?"

This time, I heard her. It was little more than a muffled sound from the kitchen, but it was enough to kick start a jolt of adrenaline through my system. I forgot my nerves and went in.

Cash hit me as soon as I crossed the threshold. I was already shaky on my feet, thanks to the past few hours, and the blow was enough to send me staggering hard into the refrigerator. I turned around to face him, to try and muster some defense on the rebound, and Cash kicked my bad leg out from underneath me. I tried to swing my cane at him, but he caught it with a mild look of amused disdain, jerked it out of my hand and began raining down blows to my head and arms. So I did what any self-respecting spell slinger would do, and curled up in a ball waiting for it to be over, which, of course, took a veritable eternity.

I finally pulled myself up to a sitting position, my back against the fridge, every inch of my body alive with pain. Melly was seated at the kitchen table, her wrists and ankles bound to one of the chairs with duct tape. She had another piece over her mouth. Even in the fading light, I could see the streaks of tears over her cheeks, an angry bruise forming under her right eye. She looked frightened, but those weren't the tears of someone who was afraid. Those were the tears of someone who was pissed off.

Cash, on the other hand, looked bored. No. Not bored, exactly. There was no emotion there.

"Jonah," he said, his voice empty. "You want to know why I don't like you?"

He pressed the point of the cane into my chest, effectively pinning me where I was sitting.

"Because you're a psychopath?" I asked.

He responded by slapping me lightly in the face with my own cane.

"Because you're a coward."

"I've been called worse," I said.

Cash didn't answer. Instead, he took a few steps back, positioning himself behind Melly. He set my cane on the table and reached out, gently, almost timidly, stroking Melly's hair. She recoiled, a movement that was equal parts disgust and rage. At that moment, I was pretty sure if her mouth wasn't taped shut she could've taken a finger off with her teeth.

"Cash," I growled. "Whatever you're thinking of doing, don't. Just don't. If you have an issue with me, then we can settle it."

Cash turned his eyes towards me, stroking Melly's hair. "You shouldn't talk," he said finally. "You should just watch."

In that moment, two things became abundantly clear. First, Cash intended to kill the both of us. Second, the pre-game show was going to be doubly horrific for Melly.

I made a decision without it really even registering that it was done. If Cash wanted to hurt Melly, or kill us, I wasn't going to make it easy.

Cash slid his hand over Melly's shoulder and to the back of her neck. Where one moment he'd been surprisingly gentle, the next he was all violence and rage. He grabbed her hair, jerking her head back, and kissed her tape-covered mouth.

Once his eyes were off of me, I launched myself at him in a full on tackle. I caught Cash perfectly, my shoulder slamming into his hips, dropping us both to the floor in a tangled mass of thrashing limbs.

Cash went absolutely ballistic. As someone who had spent several years as a thug, a few more in prison, and a lifetime of being a full-fledged asshole, he had me at a severe disadvantage. The only thing I really had going for me was the fact that in school, I'd played a whole lot of Dungeons and Dragons and could take a lot of abuse at the hands of bullies.

Cash slammed his fists into my side, peppering my ribs with quick, hard rabbit punches. Even this close, they were enough to cause my breath to catch in my chest and send slivers of pain running up and down my ribs. I tried to give it as good as I got, but it was a losing effort. The most I succeeded in doing was getting my poorly timed, weaker blows in the way of Cash's fists enough to maybe soften a shot here and there.

We scrambled on the floor for a good thirty seconds before he threw his hips up and rolled me over, planting his knee in my chest and pinning me to the floor. He punched me in the side of the head twice, each blow landing hard enough to send spots across my vision and birth a nausea-inducing pain at the base of my skull.

Once he was sure he'd taken most of the fight taken out of me, he pulled out the box cutter.

"You shouldn't have done that," he said.

"I'd planned on killing you regardless. Now, I'm just going to have to make a day out of it. You understand, right? Though, I suppose I'll keep you alive long enough that you see what happens to her," he added as an afterthought, and pressed the blade to the side of my face he hadn't carved up. I felt the blade move, and the pain a second later. Cash traced another line over my face, under my right eye and over the bridge of my nose.

He took the blade away, watching me thrash around, blood running into my eyes, with an almost clinical detachment. With him pinning me down, I could barely breathe, let alone muster up enough oxygen to scream. He waited until I finally stopped moving, and pressed the blade against the corner of my eye.

"Don't worry. Only one," he said, grabbing my hair and holding my head still. "Probably shouldn't move too much, though, you might make me miss my mark."

"Fella, I'm gonna have to ask you to be so kind as to stand up nice and slow. Otherwise, I'm gonna end up having to repaint my kitchen," came a voice from behind Cash.

Cash went perfectly still, the tip of the blade still pressed against my face, just a hair away from my eye.

"Don't make me ask you twice," my father told him, punctuating the statement with the ratcheting clack of a pump-action shotgun.

CHAPTER 17

Cash stood up slowly, taking a single step away from me.

"Now drop the box cutter and hit the floor."

I heard the clatter of the box cutter on the linoleum.

"Attaboy," my father said. "Now, Jonah, get up."

I fought back up to my feet, though it took the help of the kitchen table, and a fair bit of trying to wipe the blood out of my eyes. Once I got vertical, I wavered a bit, my head spinning from the pounding that Cash had given me.

"Old man, you have any idea the level of shit that you're—"

"Funny, I don't recall asking for your opinion," my father said. "So how about you speak when spoken to? Comprende?"

Judging from the look of surprise on Cash's face, I was pretty sure no one had talked to him like that in quite some time, if ever.

"Let me explain to you how this is going to work," my father said, as if speaking to a small child, "You're gonna turn around and leave my house and you're not going to go near my boy again."

"Yeah?"

"Yeah. Cause if you choose to do otherwise, I'm gonna hurt you," my father said. "Bad," he added.

"You got—"

"I think I told you to shut up. Now, if you want to try and see how serious I am, I'll save you the trouble. Go talk to your daddy. He knows."

I tried to wrap my head around what he'd just said. I knew my father had had a past, but to hear him talk down one of the Carvers like that shocked the hell out of me.

"Just fucking shoot him," I said.

My father turned his gaze toward me.

I'm not sure if it was the intensity of his stare, the disappointment in his eyes resonated with me. I couldn't meet his gaze. I looked at the floor, ashamed.

My father turned his attention back towards Cash, the shotgun unwavering.

"Well? What's it gonna be?" he asked.

Cash looked, for a moment, like he wanted to say something. Instead, he took a few more steps backward, then turned and bolted out of the house. My father lowered the shotgun, watching the door after he'd gone.

"Don't just stand there bleeding on the floor, boy, untie the lady," he said finally, propping the shotgun up in the corner. "I'll go get the first aid kit and patch you up."

I blinked once, the new cut on my face burning. I didn't think it was too deep, but it hurt like hell and I could feel the blood drying on my cheek. I scooped up the cutter, and after a minute or two of work, managed to cut Melly free.

She shot to her feet and I had to grab her around the waist to keep her from bolting out the door and chasing Cash down.

"Easy, killer," I said.

After a bout of cursing that would be considered impressive in even the rowdiest of company, she finally calmed down and turned towards me.

"Jesus, Jonah. Your face."

"I am a pretty man, aren't I?"

"What the hell were you thinking?" she snapped, slamming a fist against my shoulder. "He could've killed you!"

"Go easy on the boy," my father said, walking back into the kitchen and setting the first aid kit on the table. "He wasn't lucky enough to inherit my brains."

Melly glowered at me, then took a step back, her anger still barely in check. After a moment, she looked between me and my father.

"Shouldn't he go to the hospital?" she asked.

"Nope," my father said. "Doesn't make a whole lot of sense for him to owe a hospital a few thousand dollars when I can do it for free."

He walked over to the counter, washed his hands, and started a pot of coffee, then sat down at the kitchen table and opened the kit. He sorted through the contents, setting a few things out on the table.

"Cash is gonna be pissed. Best to let him calm down before you go anywhere else, Jonah," my father said. "Once I get you put back together, me and you need to have a conversation."

My father gave me that look again, the one that made me feel about a quarter of an inch tall.

Melly paced back and forth, all but fuming.

"We should call the police," she said.

"Wouldn't do any good. Anything short of murder, the cops aren't gonna give the Carvers the time of day. Too much pull," my father said. "Sit down, Jonah. Let me take a look."

I sat down in a chair opposite of my old man. He sat down and gave my face the once over, using a wet towel to wipe away the blood.

"Ain't as bad as it looks, but I'll still have to stitch it up," he said, after a moment's appraisal. "Probably gonna hurt like hell."

"I don't suppose you have any Novocain in there?"

"I think you're numb enough," he said, a hint of displeasure lining his words.

"Yeah, well, given the way my day's going," I said, letting my voice trail off.

He ignored me, turning his attention to Melly and his kit.

"Mind giving me a hand?" he asked.

"I'm not exactly a nurse," she said.

"Well, that works out then. I ain't no doctor," he said.

Melly looked between my father and me, then shrugged.

"What the hell?"

Melly pulled a chair up next to my father and sat down. He poked and prodded around the wound with his finger, his fingertips rough with calluses.

"Hand me that gauze, damn thing's bleeding like hell."

Melly handed him the gauze, and he once more mopped blood from my face. The pain, once sharp, had become a dull, burning throb. He pressed the gauze to my face, sopping up more blood, and he did it none too gently.

"There's a suture kit," he said. "Bottom of the kit."

Melly dug around a bit until she found it and handed it to him. He tore the little sterilization wrapper off with his teeth and spit it on the floor. He fixed the little curved needle into a set of clamps and held it up to the light, sizing it up, before placing the point against my skin.

"You ready?" he asked.

"I—"

He didn't wait for me to finish answering. Instead, he pushed the needle through my skin, dragging the thread through behind it. Without missing a beat, he looped the thread around and pulled the stitch tight, tying it off.

"Scissors?"

Melly handed him the scissors and he clipped it off. He repeated the process another sixteen times, and before it was all said and done, I'd almost gotten used to it. When he was done, he cut a strip of gauze, applied some antibiotic cream to it and taped it to my face. He even changed the dressing on the other cut, his surprise evident when he realized I'd managed to keep all of those stitches intact. Once he was finished, my father stowed the gear back in his case and vanished down the hallway.

I had a cup of coffee waiting for him when he got back. He took it without saying a word and went through the small door in the kitchen that led to the back porch. I made a cup for myself, then followed him outside.

"Leg's bothering you again, huh?" my father asked. He didn't bother turning around when I'd stepped out, he just stood there, staring into the backyard.

"Yeah, rough couple of days," I said.

He nodded, settling his mug on the railing. He pulled a pipe from his pocket, an old briar that he'd had since I was a kid and started packing it full with tobacco. Once it was loaded to his satisfaction, he clamped it in his teeth and lit it with a wooden match.

"Jonah, you mind if I ask you something?" he said after a few minutes of silence. There was hesitation in his voice. Whatever was on his mind was heavy.

My father didn't know what I was, or what I was capable of. It was the one secret I'd managed to keep from him for years. I don't think it was a fear he wouldn't believe me. Hell, I don't even know if he'd care one way or the other. There was just something inside of me that kept me from spilling, an irrational fear that I couldn't put my finger on.

"Yeah, what's up, Pop?"

"What the hell are you into, Son?" he asked, the question wrapped up in the sigh of a man who was setting down a heavy burden.

I closed my eyes, sighed, and set my coffee on the railing, taking up a spot beside him.

"It's a long story," I said.

"I'm sure, but from where I'm sitting it looks like you got roped into something."

"Suppose that's one way to look at it."

"I'm guessing that rope's just about the right length for you to hang yourself, too."

"That about sums it up," I admitted.

"Uh-huh," he said, poking at the tobacco in his pipe with the tip of his matchstick. "So what're the cliff notes?"

I wanted to tell him something, anything, that would

ease his worry, but I didn't know what I could say that would do that. So, I went with the truth. Sort of.

"I got involved with some bad people. I'm just trying to get out."

"Right," my father said, eyeing the bandages. "Well, you're obviously doing a stellar job."

"Obviously," I said, the joke falling flat.

"Yeah? So what about whatever it is you're involved with sounded like a good idea at the time?"

"The follies of youth?" I said with a shrug.

"Too drunk to think?" he suggested. I didn't answer.

He relit his pipe, took a few puffs and exhaled in a long, slow sigh.

"I'm gonna be straight with you, son," he said. "For the last year or so, I been watching you drink yourself to death. It's my fault. I ain't said nothing, and I should've, God knows I should've. Hell, I was hoping you'd figure it on your own, but damn it, boy, you need help."

"Wait. What?"

"You heard me, Jonah. You got a problem. I don't even think you see it."

"Oh, for crying out loud, Pop."

"Don't."

"Seriously? Who the hell do you think you are?" I asked, my ire rising.

"I'm your father, Jonah, and you're a god damned drunk. Whether you see it or not, I do, and I'm not going to watch it anymore. Hell, I can't," he said, turning his attention back to the yard. He held his pipe like he didn't know if he wanted to smoke it or throw it, before finally locking it between his teeth again and taking a few rapid puffs.

"This is bullshit," I said, finally.

"Really? Cause the son I know, my son, he wouldn't be in this kind of shit. He's too smart to get involved with the Carvers and he's damn sure too smart to let them get the better of him."

"I—"

"No, Jonah. Not another word. Here's the situation. I'm gonna let you stay here tonight, give that Carver boy a bit of time to cool off, like I said. After that, you ain't coming back here until you start getting yourself some help."

"Wait. What?"

"You heard me," my father said, turning his attention back towards me. "If your mother, hell, if Gretchen could see you right now," he said, his voice trailing off.

"So it's just going to be like that?"

My father wiped his eyes absently with the back of his hand.

"Yeah, unfortunately it is," he said.

For the next few minutes, neither of us said anything.

"So, we clear?" he asked me, finally.

"Crystal," I growled.

My father nodded once, turned, and went inside, leaving me standing alone on the porch.

CHAPTER 18

I stood on the porch for a long time, staring up at the sky, losing myself as the last of the sunset melted away, the reds and purples fading into a starlit darkness. I didn't want to think about what my father had said, but I felt uncomfortable going back in and facing him. My coffee had long since gone cold, which was fine. I'd all but forgotten it anyways. There was no reason for what he said to bother me. It was utter crap. My father was just being over protective. I was in some shit, and probably in over my head. Hell, he'd come home and found some crazed nutbag in his house beating the bejesus out of his kid. That was enough to make anyone try and lay blame somewhere.

But I'd done it for him. If it weren't for me, he'd have lost his business, his livelihood.

"How's your face," Melly asked, stepping onto the back porch. She had a fresh mug of coffee, which she carried over and set down on the banister next to me. She picked up my cup from earlier, dumped it out, then held the mug loosely in one hand, arms crossed over her chest.

"Attached. Mostly, anyways," I said.

I wasn't really in the mood for company. I picked up the coffee from the railing and took a sip. Say what you will about Melly, she was a wonder when it came to making just about any form of consumable liquid.

"Well, that's something," she said.

"Yeah, I suppose it is."

"So this is where you grew up, huh?"

"Yeah. Well, sort of. We lived in Oregon for a little while, then New Orleans, both before my sister died. It's mostly been here, though, for about as long as I can remember. Guess a better way to put it is that it's all I remember."

She nodded.

"It's nice."

"Yeah, maybe. It's not all happy memories, though. Lot of bad happened here, too. I guess that's what makes it home."

"That tends to be how it works," Melly agreed. "I wanted to say thanks."

"For?"

"Everything you and your dad have done. I appreciate it. Especially your dad. He's a character."

"That's one way to put it."

"Seriously, thanks," she said again.

"Yeah, don't mention it."

There was a long, awkward pause.

"I wanted to thank you for not blowing up in there, too," she added.

"What do you mean?" I asked.

"When I was talking about…about what happened."

I nodded.

"Didn't seem right. Doesn't mean it doesn't bother me, but," I shrugged. "I don't know. I'm just glad you're okay."

"Yeah," she said. "I get it."

"Good, cause I'm not a hundred percent sure I do."

She snickered.

"It means a lot."

I nodded.

"Look, not to be rude, I'm not really in the mood for chit chat right now."

"I know," she said. "Still, wanted to say my piece."

"I'm sorry," I said finally.

"Don't be."

"Just not a good time," I admitted.

"Anything you want to talk about?"

"Not really."

"You sure?"

I wasn't. I wanted to get it off my chest. The problem was, I wasn't sure exactly what it was. There was something that bothered me about what my dad said, about everything, but I didn't know how to quantify it. I couldn't make sense of it enough to put words to it, let alone vocalize it.

"I don't know," I said finally.

"I been there," she said, leaning her elbow on the rails and staring down into the yard.

"I doubt that," I said.

"I don't."

I took another long sip of coffee.

"I'm not gonna push it. If you wanna talk, we can talk.

It's the least I can do after all this. If you don't, well, that's on you," she said, finally.

"Yeah," I said, a little harsher than I had intended. "Thanks."

Melly nodded and turned, heading back inside. The door shut behind her loudly. I looked back up to the stars and couldn't help but wish, not for the first time, that Gretchen was here. She'd walked me through so much, helped me get a handle on things that I couldn't comprehend when I was just a kid. After my mother had left, she was the closest thing I'd had to any sort of maternal figure. She'd know how to handle all of this nonsense.

When I finally decided to move, I took the long way around the house, heading out front to my truck. I wasn't entirely sure what I was going to do, but I had few ideas on how I could kill some time until I figured it out. I had the runestone piece and the two books I'd stolen from Mama Duvalier. Given that I was strongly outgunned at the moment, I needed to try and drum up some leverage.

Unfortunately, all I had was Gus.

Gus was sort of the go to when it came to the weird. He made a decent enough living fencing trinkets, books, relics, and all kinds of other magic doohickeys that really only had any value to a very small, very select clientele.

He was also a paranoid conspiracy theorist.

I took a few minutes once I was situated in my truck to grab a few swigs from the bottle of rum I'd taken with my plunder and snap some pictures of my haul before I called Gus.

The phone rang once.

"This line isn't secure," he said and hung up. No "hello."

No, "Jonah, it's been a while." Nothing but good old-fashioned trademark Gus crazy. It was kind of comforting.

A moment later, he called back. I let it ring a few times before I answered.

"Jonah," he said.

"Gus."

"What?"

"I'm going to send you some pictures. Items I need to help—"

"No, you're not," he snapped, cutting me off.

"I—"

"Don't care. No pictures. Bring whatever it is to me," he said, and hung up again.

I sighed, started my girl up and put the truck in gear.

CHAPTER 19

Gus lived maybe forty, forty-five minutes outside Asheville, near some little no name incorporated town in the middle of nowhere.

I'd helped Gus out with a few things way back when and technically he owed me a favor or two. Thankfully, his line of work meant that he was very clued into the supernatural world. Granted, he was also firmly convinced that all the bad things out of storybooks—the monsters, vampires, Fae, werewolves, spirits, and gods from mythology—were all involved in running some sort of shadowy shadow government. He also believed that said shadowy shadow government operated solely on the need to turn the entirety of the human race into slaves, food, or both.

Gus lived in a farmhouse at the end of a long gravel road, isolated from the rest of civilization. The entire perimeter, roughly a few acres, was surrounded by a make-shift fence made mostly out of wooden pallets, old road signs, vinyl siding, and the occasional dilapidated car.

I pulled up to the gate, which was set a good half mile from the house, and rolled down the window. A small security camera tracked my every move, a little bit of tech that stood out against the hodge podge of the fence. After a moment, the gate started sliding open and Gus's voice came from an as of yet unseen speaker.

"Leave the truck," it said.

I rolled my eyes.

"I saw that," the voice added.

I sighed, killed the ignition and hopped out of the truck, my bag over my shoulder, the bottle hanging loosely from one hand, my cane in the other.

As I trekked along the long gravel drive, I took in the land around me. Given the amount of spotlights he had trained on just about every last inch of the property, it was frighteningly easy. All in all, it would have been picturesque if the grass wasn't knee high, full of brambles, rampant tangles of blackberry bushes, fallen branches from past storms, and more than a handful of cleverly hidden booby traps. A few trees, mostly massive oaks and willows, dotted the landscape. In the distance, I could see a small field, set just to the side of the house. Wooden boxes, beehives, were lined up in perfect little rows, five wide and five deep in the field. Somewhere in the distance, I could hear the chugging of a diesel generator.

By the time I made it to the porch, I felt like I'd hiked my way up a mountain. The porch itself was on the verge of collapse and littered with old lawnmower parts, a chainsaw or two, a few metal ammo boxes, gas cans, and various other random junk, from pink lawn flamingos to extension cords to yard gnomes.

I reached out to knock on the steel-plated door and Gus's voice sprang to life from another intercom.

"Don't. It's live."

"What?"

A little slot opened in the door and a set of eyes peered out. They were bloodshot, with heavy bags underneath them.

"The door's live."

"Live? What the hell do you mean live?" I asked.

"It means if you touch this door before I disarm the security system, you won't be." He slid the little trap door shut. I heard a few noises from the other side, then the trap door opened again.

"There. Come on in."

Gus's castle of paranoia was a study in psychosis. He'd gutted the interior down to the wall studs, leaving the wiring and plumbing exposed to the open air. There were about twenty-five car batteries wired together and attached to the door with jumper cables running along the wall by the door. I understood what he meant about the term live, now. Thankfully, one of the terminals had been unhooked. If I'd grabbed the door before he'd unhooked it, I'd have been able to power a small city. The lighting came, mostly, from shop and work lights running off the generator I heard outside. He led me into what had probably once been a living room, where he did the majority of his work. There were six TVs in one corner, mounted to the wall studs, each one playing a different major news outlet. Next to that, was what I can only assume was some sort of server computer. Whatever it was, it had a lot of flashing lights, whirring fans, big metal boxes and brightly colored cables. There was a desk and rather fancy-looking office chair next to that. Computer monitors were mounted over the desk, the top of which held two keyboards and roughly a hundred empty food containers of various stripes, ethnicities, and shall we say, freshness.

What boggled my mind the most was the sheer number of photographs, newspaper articles, magazine articles, and computer printouts stapled, tacked, and taped to every exposed wall stud, the ceiling and, in some cases the floor. There had to have been roughly a mile and a half of string connecting them all.

"I see you've redecorated," I said.

"Blow it out your ass, Jonah," Gus said, shuffling over to his desk chair, dropping down into it, and staring up at the various monitors. That was how we usually greeted each other.

Gus was a big guy, pushing four hundred pounds, with a mop of black hair and a thick shadow of stubble over his cheeks. He wore bright blue basketball shorts and a long sleeve flannel shirt, which was buttoned all wrong. To be fair, when you never leave the house, fashion stops being a priority. He plucked a pair of glasses off the desk and put them on, peered up at one of the monitors, punched a few keys on his keyboard, nodded smugly, and then settled back into his chair.

"You look like hell, by the way," he said.

"Thanks," I said. "Long day."

"Is there any other kind?"

"Not in my experience."

"So, what brings you to my neck of the woods?"

"I need some help."

"So you said. What kind of help?"

"I need to unload a couple of books, one of them is a summoning book. I'm not really too sure on the who's or the what's. I'm going to need the skinny on a hunk of rock, too."

"Hunk of rock?"

"Woman wants it bad enough to pay me four figures. It's got a little something to it, but I wanna know what."

"Well, show me what you got."

I pulled out my phone, flipped it to the pictures I'd taken and tossed it to him. He caught it, turned to his desk, and hooked it up to some wire. A second later, a grid of pictures of popped up on the monitor. Gus opened the first image, the summoning book, the picture filling the entirety of one of his screens.

Gus whistled.

"Where did you find this?" he asked.

"You sure you want to know?"

"Hit me."

"Stole it from Mama Duvalier."

Gus blinked.

"I'm sorry?"

"You heard me," I said, a hint of pride coloring my tone.

"Are you absolutely brain dead?" he asked.

I shrugged.

"Mind if I take a look?"

I pulled the book out of my bag and handed it to him. He opened it at random, placed it on a photo scanner, and let the machine do its thing. While it did that, he pulled up the picture of the next book, stared at it for a moment, then slid over to the next picture, the piece of stone that Lysone had wanted me to procure.

"Huh," he said, more to himself than to me. "That's …huh."

Gus settled back into his chair.

"I'm gonna need a little time for this one," he said, nodding towards the screen. "The first book, too. The other one is just a codex. Nothing too fancy. I can get you a few hundred bucks for it."

"That works," I said.

"Give me a few minutes to work," he said, stretching his arms and cracking his knuckles like the world's most disheveled concert pianist.

I paced around Gus's place. Every now and again, I'd stop and peer at some of his pictures and connections. It would seem, in Gus's worldview, there was a connection between the United Nations, the Kardashians, a small earthquake in Siberia, and the collapse of a small Internet provider in Wisconsin. This in turn branched off to a swarm of Killer Bees in Africa, the sinking of a cargo ship off the coast of Taiwan, and the death from drunk driving of two sorority girls in Tucson.

"Oooh, well now we're getting somewhere," Gus said from somewhere over my shoulder.

"What'd you find?"

"Huh? Nothing."

I shook my head and went back to tracing my way through Gus's web of conspiracy. Honestly, after about fifteen minutes, some of it made a little bit of sense. Not a lot. Just enough to make me start wondering about my own sanity.

You know, in case the prior thirty-six hours wasn't enough.

"Alright, got it," Gus said.

I walked over to him and peered at the monitors over his shoulder. He reeked of sweat, but my presence there made him a little uncomfortable, so I stuck it out. You know, for my own amusement. Gus stared up at me, narrowed his eyes in a glare, then turned back to his own privatized version of NORAD.

"You want the intel on the book or the stone first?" he asked.

"Book."

"Alright, from what I can tell the book originated in the Appalachians," Gus said, punching a few keys. "You can tell by some of the writing. It has a very distinct vernacular. Also, if you look at the leather of the cover, which is absolutely beautiful—"

"Appreciate the assessment of its artistic value, but that's not really what I'm looking for."

"Alright, you want the dirt. I get it. Here's the skinny thus far: the book's a summoning book. Mostly Fae, from what I can tell. Heavy hitters too, named stuff. Sort of a rolodex of badasses. There's some other stuff in some Scandinavian runic language, Russian, a little bit of Greek, but it's mostly Fae."

"You can move it?"

"For the normal fee."

"Done. What about the rock?"

"Well now, that one's interesting. It would seem what you have in your hands is a hunk of the Ledberg stone."

"A runestone. Yeah, I know."

"Right, scholars argue over what it depicts. Either it's the end of the world or some poor bastard getting beaten in a fight. Point is, a piece is missing. You have that missing piece so you can finally answer that question once and for all, if you're into that kind of thing."

"I'm not. What's it worth?"

"In the right hands, a lot."

"More than five K?"

"Oh yeah, a lot more."

"Excellent."

"There's more."

I quirked a brow.

"Well, don't keep me in suspense."

"If you look here," he said, tapping an image on the screen with a dirty chopstick, "You see those marks?"

I nodded.

"Those are inscriptions. They're time-worn, almost to the point of being indecipherable, but they're there."

"Okay? And?"

"Give me a day, maybe two, give or take, I can probably track it all down and tell you what it means. It could be something that'll up the value or it could be Great Aunt Helga's mead recipe."

"Sure, why not? Let's chalk it up to academic curiosity."

"In other words, you want to see if you can squeeze more money out of your buyer," Gus said.

"Basically," I said.

"Fair enough," he said.

"Alright, Gus, work your magic. I'm gonna step outside, make a call."

"You can't."

"Uh, okay?"

"You need to go at least two miles in any direction."

"What?"

"Cell phone jammers," he explained. "I have them strategically placed to limit communications. You'll need to drive at least two miles to get out of their radius."

I blinked.

"You put in cell phone jammers?"

"And RF Frequency blockers, some homemade thermal dampening. Oh, and carbon monoxide detectors. I work in mysterious ways."

"Right. Of course you do. Can't be too safe, right? Call me when you have something?"

"Sure," Gus said, getting back to his typing and forgetting about me almost instantly.

CHAPTER 20

I called Lysone on the way back to Asheville and hoped to God I didn't pass a cop. I had a bottle of rum in one hand, was trying to dial a cell phone with the other, all while trying to steer with one knee. At the moment, I figured I was pretty much the poster boy for poor driving decisions.

Once more, she answered the phone before it even rang. I had to admit, it was more than a little creepy.

"Mister Heywood," she said, voice cool, calm, and collected, every last syllable all business.

"I have your rock."

There was a pause that lasted so long I thought she'd hung up on me.

"You have it?" she asked.

"I do."

"Where would you like me to meet you?" she asked, and something in her voice had changed. There was an anticipation there, something bordering on desperation. It set my nerves on edge. I'd hear that sort of tone in addicts who needed a fix and weren't above doing very bad things to get right.

"Are you opposed to meeting me at Jack of the Wood?" I asked.

"It's not my preference," she admitted.

"Good. Meet me there in say, two hours?"

"Are you sure that's the proper venue?"

"Sure enough that that's where we're going."

"If I must."

"You must. Two hours."

"Why the delay?"

"Because I've had a really long, really shitty day and I'd like a shower," I said, catching a quick glimpse of my face in the rearview. I actually wasn't sure a shower was going to cover it. A few specks of dried blood still hung to my cheek, mixed in with a fair amount of smudged grime. My hair was standing up at angles that were most likely only found in some kind of Lovecraftian geometry. Heavy bags had collected under my eyes, my skin had a washed-out, pale, cast. Overall, I just looked like utter crap.

"I see."

"God, I hope not," I muttered under my breath.

"Excuse me," she said.

"Nothing. Two hours, Jack of the Wood. Doable?"

"Very. Do not be late, Mister Heywood," she said and hung up.

I tossed the phone onto the seat beside me and turned into my trailer park. The trailers, most of them already in varying states of disrepair, had a looming, almost graveyard-like quality. Maybe it was the dilapidated cars in the driveways, their hoods left open to the night sky. Maybe it was the unkempt lawns, forgotten toys, and tarped-over riding lawnmowers. Either way, home base seemed creepier than usual.

I pulled into my driveway, shoved my bag under the seat, locked the doors, and trudged inside. Given that I was only walking about twenty, maybe thirty feet total, I left my cane in the truck as well. If I needed it, I had more inside.

Once I entered, I stripped down and hopped in the shower, taking care not to get the veritable army of stitches holding my face together wet. The water was glorious. Say what you will about my little shanty, but the water heater was awesome. I had to replace the element more than once, and I'd finally decided to put in one that didn't exactly meet specifications. It blew the breaker, more often than not, but it was pure, molten, scalding goodness after a long day. I closed my eyes and reveled in it, letting the water beat at my aching muscles.

I was midway through my shower when the power went out. There's vulnerable, and then there's standing in a two by two stall, naked, soaking wet, and covered with lavender and green tea scented soap suds vulnerable. I was horribly, frighteningly vulnerable.

I stood stock still until my heart rate returned to normal, turned off the water, and took in the sudden silence. There was no hum of floorboard heaters, no ticking or whirring from the refrigerator, nothing. Just an eerie quiet that seemed to settle over everything with an oppressive weight.

I pushed the stall door open, stepped into the bathroom, and started feeling around blindly for a towel and my clothes. It took a minute, but I managed to dry off and get dressed without falling over, knocking something down, or stepping into the toilet. Of course, that feeling of relief slipped away like sand when I heard the steps on the front porch and the screen door open and shut.

There was a chance that it could've been one of my neighbors stopping by to check about the power. It could've been Rick, the cable guy who lived in the trailer next door coming to tell me about his most recent service call turned bored housewife rendezvous. Or, it could've been Sherri, the stripper. Somehow, I doubted it was any of them. Call it a hunch, the law of probability, or hell, call it the fact that everyone I'd met over the past forty-eight hours had tried to kill me, but I wasn't feeling confident that things weren't, once again, going completely pear shaped.

I was in a trailer bathroom, with one exit that led into a small, cramped hallway, no cover, and walls that were about as thick as construction paper. The only window in the room was roughly four inches tall by twenty-four inches long, far too small to serve as an exit. As far as weaponry went, I had a bottle of shampoo, a cheap dollar store razor, a plunger, and a few bottles of over the counter medicines.

I couldn't sit in the bathroom all night, nor could I make my presence known. So, I cracked the door and stuck my head out, ever so slowly.

In retrospect, it probably wasn't the most sound or well thought out strategy.

I saw a shadow, a blur of movement. After that the lights, both metaphorical and literal, went out.

CHAPTER 21

The first thing I saw, when I opened my eyes, was stars. Not the cute little animated stars like in the cartoons, but real stars dotting a night sky far overhead. After that came the pain. This time it was a nauseating, skull-wrenching headache. Just turning my head made me feel like I was going to violently expel any food I'd recently eaten. I could feel a patch of heat against my back, not painful, but warm enough that it was uncomfortable. A moment later, the rumbling of an engine filtered in, followed by the vibration of motion and the occasional bone-jarring bump. My arms were bound behind me, and judging from how wide the bindings felt, it was probably duct tape. I tried to move my legs and found them stuck together at the ankle, no doubt bound with the same roll of tape.

It took a minute for me to sort through the varying sensations, but I eventually came to the realization that I was in the bed of a truck. Then the familiar rhythm of the engine struck me, and I realized I was in the bed of my truck.

I cannot even begin to put into words exactly how much this pissed me off. If I'd had a girlfriend, I'd be less upset if I'd caught the mystery driver in bed with her.

I tried to sit up, but whoever was driving was obviously paying attention, because as soon as I made the attempt, the truck swerved hard to the right, slamming me back down to the sheet metal and sending me sliding across the bed.

"Oh c'mon," I muttered. "Alright, think Heywood."

My bag was still in the truck. The stuff inside of it would be pretty damned useful if I stood a snowball's chance in hell of actually getting to it. Given my situation, I had a feeling that that was becoming increasingly unlikely. I had to figure out a way to work with what I had.

I took a quick stock of the crap in the back of my truck. There were some pine needles, which would be absolutely awesome if I wanted to purge my truck of negative energies. There was a whole crap ton of acorns, which, given the fact that I wasn't having fertility issues, were useless. If I'd had more time, I could use them to make a protection charm. Since there wasn't a hostile spirit driving my girl and holding me hostage, that wouldn't really do me any good either. The tire iron was in the cab. That left me with a few empty fast food bags, a gas can, and about a hundred empty beer cans of varying vintage to work with.

The truck jerked to the side, sliding me across the bed in the opposite direction, and the sound of tires on pavement was replaced with the crunching of gravel. Where the sky had been open only moments ago, trees now stood in my periphery, throwing spires of shadow against an already dark sky.

Whatever I was going to do, I was going to have to do it really quick.

I rolled around in the bed of the truck, grasping blindly until I felt my fingers close around one of the beer cans. It took me a minute to get it flatted out, given that I couldn't get that much leverage with my hands taped together. Once I'd flattened the can, I started working it back and forth until the aluminum tore. Once it ripped and I had a makeshift blade, I started hacking at the tape as best I could.

The trees around me blotted out the stars and cast even more shadow across the back of the truck, which had slowed to a crawl. The bumps were hitting harder and more frequently now.

I was halfway through the tape when the truck came to a stop. The door opened, slammed shut, and a moment later Cash Carver was standing beside the bed of my truck, his elbows resting on the sheet metal, staring at me.

I wish I could say I was surprised.

"Hello Jonah," he said, twirling my keys around his finger, before slipping them into his pocket.

"Cash," I said, rolling up onto my side, holding my makeshift blade in my hands. "Judging from our situation, I'm guessing you're a little miffed right about now."

"I'm not pleased, no."

"I'm guessing you wouldn't be interested in a conversation of some sort? Maybe a bit of parlay?"

Cash stared at me.

"No? You sure?"

That same dead stare.

"Cash, listen to me. You kill me, you don't get your money," I said, trying to keep a rapidly growing note of panic out of my voice.

"Surprisingly, that's not entirely a concern of mine at the moment. You have something of mine already."

"I do? Want to share what that is?"

"When I was younger," Cash explained, ignoring my question. "My Uncle's neighbor had cats. A lot of cats."

"Uh, okay?" I said, trying my best to saw at my bonds as inconspicuously as possible. For the time being at least, it seemed, it was working.

"I stayed up there during the summer every year," Cash explained, his voice strangely nostalgic, almost wistful. "These cats, they were in heat a lot. Always yowling and carrying on. Kept me awake more nights than I can count."

"They do that," I agreed.

"They do. It drove me crazy," he said.

"Oh, so that was it. I thought it was daddy issues."

Cash ignored me.

"So, one day, I get an idea. I'm going to make them stop and I'm finally going to get some damned sleep," he said, staring off into the distance. "So, that's what I set out to do. First, I got me a possum trap. One of them cages with the little snap-down door. Possum goes in, starts eating the bait, and the door shuts. Very humane. Once they're caught, you take them out in the woods and set them free. The problem is, animals have a way of finding their way back home."

Cash pulled a lighter out of his pocket and absently started flipping the top open and shut while he talked.

"I caught the first one. He was a little thing, real scrawny, with black and white fur. He kind of looked like he was wearing a tux. So, I had this kitten in a cage, and I needed to figure out how to shut it up, cause when I caught it, it just screamed and screamed. So I got to thinking—"

"Well that can't be good."

He kept on with his story; I kept trying to cut my tape.

"My uncle, when he wasn't kicking the crap out of my cousins, he used to fix lawnmowers and the like for folks. It helped him get beer money. He used to always keep a can of gasoline in the shed out back, mostly just for cleaning parts. So I got that gas can, stole a book of matches out of the house, and took the cat down to the creek. I dumped the gas on him, set a match to him. He howled then, with good reason, I suppose, but in the end, he finally got quiet."

"You're a sick fuck," I said, finally.

Cash sighed.

"Well, I'm about to do the same thing to you."

CHAPTER 22

Cash paced around to the back of my truck, tapping his lighter against the finish as he went.

He dropped the tailgate and hopped up into the back with me. With Cash standing over me, I stopped working at the tape and clenched my hands around my homemade blade. He took a step towards me and I squirmed away from him, pressing my back against the back of the truck's cab. I shot out both feet in a hard kick, aiming at his kneecap. He sidestepped the blow, shaking his head with mild annoyance.

"Don't fight," Cash said.

When I tried to kick him again he caught my ankles and took a few steps back, dragging me right off the back of the truck and to the dirt. I hit the ground hard enough that my breath got caught somewhere between my stomach and lungs in a hard, leaden ball. The torn can in my hand cut into my palm. The impact dazed me enough that I barely felt it while Cash started to drag me across the ground, finally turning me loose a good twenty feet away from my truck.

"Wait here," he said and turned, trudging back towards my truck.

I sawed furiously at the tape around my wrist with my makeshift shiv. It took a second, but I felt the tension snap and my hands came mostly free. Cash had his back to me, and I took that opportunity to finally free both hands, working the fingers to get the blood flowing. I was laying on my back, in the dirt, my head hurt, my hands hurt. Hell, I hurt all over.

But I had a plan.

Well, not a plan.

More like half a plan.

Okay, it was an idea at best.

Fine. Long shot.

Alright, I admit. What I was about to do, I saw it in a movie once.

Cash grabbed the gas can out of the back of my truck and walked back towards me, unscrewed the cap, and dumped a trail of gas on the ground as he went. The smell of it, overly sweet and chemical, struck me hard. Now that I could smell the gas, hear it splash over the ground, the threat of death somehow became tangible. It took everything I had to not crawl away.

Cash walked the trail of gasoline over to me, then splashed it over my legs and feet. The smell of it hit me harder, to the point that I could taste it.

I threw a handful of dirt and gravel into Cash's face. It didn't exactly work like the movies, but it did the job. Cash dropped the gas can, swatting and wiping at his eyes. I tore at the tape around my ankles, freeing them.

I couldn't take him in a fistfight, I'd already learned that from experience. My little distraction would buy me a second, maybe three. I got to my feet, and opted out of playing fair all together.

I kicked him as hard as I could, right in the manbits.

Cash dropped to his knees, hands over his junk, his face streaked with dirt. I grabbed the gas can and swung it, using the extra weight of the gallon or two of gas for added momentum, and clocked him in the side of the head with it. There was a hollow thud and Cash fell over, onto his side. The weight of the can kept me spinning, throwing me off balance and sending me back into the dirt and dousing the both of us with even more gasoline.

"That was uncalled for, Jonah," Cash said. Other than sounding a little winded, he didn't seem to be suffering too much in the way of ill effects.

My keys were in his pocket, which made trying to drive away pretty useless since going near Cash seemed like a bad idea. Instead, I got to my feet and ran to my truck, yanking my bag out from the seat and then turned, bolting towards the trees as fast as my one and a half pins would carry me.

I hit the woods at a stumbling run, low lying branches slapping me in the face, tendrils of underbrush tearing at my legs. I sucked in big, hulking gulps of air as I went, each breath smelling like dirt and pine and forest and the ever-present scent of the gasoline that was soaking my clothes.

I wasn't much of a runner, or hell, much of an anything physical, so I started getting winded quick. I figured I had a few minutes' lead, at best, on Cash. I ducked behind a tree and tried to remain still long enough to catch my breath. Behind me, I heard Cash's pursuit. He was moving slow and methodical, and I suddenly understood how a rabbit feels with the hounds baying at its heels.

I needed to make the best of what little time I had before Cash tracked me down. When he'd caught me in my old man's house, and at my place, I'd been naked. That wasn't the case this time. This time, I had my bag of tricks with me.

I opened my bag and start rummaging, as quickly and quietly as I could. I needed to incapacitate him long enough to get my keys out of his pocket and get to my truck. Unfortunately, I didn't think a dose of Valerian like I'd given Sam would do the trick. I had a few things to work with, nothing fatal or that would cause lasting harm, but enough that an idea was starting to take shape.

I bit down on my lip until I tasted blood, then spit in the palm of my hand. I took a deep breath, steeled my nerves, and stepped out from behind the tree. Cash's head snapped towards me, and I could see his outline moving towards me through the trees and underbrush. He stopped a few feet away from where I was standing, and even in the darkness, I could see the tire iron from my truck in his right hand.

"I wish you hadn't made me traipse through the woods after you."

"So I was supposed to lay there and let you burn me alive?"

"Mostly, yes."

"You know what? To hell with you, Cash. To hell with

your brother. To hell with your daddy, and your little thug friends and your ugly Cadillac and just your whole incestual backwoods mafia wanna-be family."

Cash didn't say anything. Instead, he started towards me with a stomping urgency, which was exactly what I'd hoped for. I tossed the fetish I'd taken out of my bag, a large hunk of quartz with a spirit bound inside it, from one hand to the other. I felt the spirit inside it stir as soon as the blood staining my palm touched the outside of the fetish.

Spirits are, essentially, thought forms. In other words, when a person thinks of say, a wolf, they create an image in their mind. In the spirit world, all these images from different people start to take form, shape, and substance. They reflect the beliefs of people in general. So, said wolf for example, would be the sum of man's take on wolves. They'd be big, beautiful, terrifyingly savage creatures that, compared to modern wolves, would look like something out of the Paleozoic Era. That was because mankind, over millennia, had feared wolves and admired them. Their form would reflect that collected belief.

Spirits don't really happen a lot in the material world. They don't mix well, the two different planes. The vast majority of spirits can't cross over to the physical plane of existence without some sort of help. Keeping them here, be it via circle or fetish, was a different animal altogether. A circle, as long as it was made right, could hold just about anything. Problem was, circles weren't portable. Fetishes were. They were a lot harder to construct, a lot more violent when they failed, and a lot more entertaining if you could turn that failure in someone else's direction. Circles were like putting a muzzle on a friendly dog. Cracking open a fetish was like giving Cujo a shot of crystal meth and a direction.

It would take the spirit a second or two to break from the fetish now that it was charged it up with my blood. Once free, the spirit would only manifest for a second or two before it dematerialized, vanishing back into the spirit world. Given what I had trapped in the quartz, I was pretty sure a second or two would do the job.

I threw the quartz at Cash and turned my back to him. There was a loud pop and the woods lit up with brilliant, white light. There was a sound sort of like sizzling grease for a brief second and then everything went dark again, the light spirit vanishing back to its home plane of existence.

I turned back around and, even though I hadn't been caught by the spiritual flashbang, it still took a second for my vision to adjust to the dark. Cash hadn't been so lucky. He'd caught the spirit's light show full frontal and it had, in turn, effectively blinded him. Cash was on his knees, one hand over his eyes, the other feeling the ground around him, trying to compensate for a lost sense. I grabbed the first thing I could find and came back with a large stick, roughly as thick as my wrist and as long as I was tall. I swung with both hands. There was a dull thud, the makeshift club connecting with Cash's ribs, just under his arm. I heard him exhale in a massive whoosh and fall over. I hit him again, this time in the hips, then again, and again, over and over again until my makeshift club finally snapped. When it was all said and done, Cash lay on the ground, motionless.

I took the opportunity, shot over to Cash, fished my keys out of his pockets and ran for my life.

CHAPTER 23

The climb back out of the woods was worse than when I went in, partially due to the fact that my eyes still hadn't adjusted fully to the darkness. I tripped and stumbled over exposed roots, falling once into a tangle of thorny vines. When I finally made it back to the car, the smell of gasoline assaulted my senses, reminding me of what I'd just escaped. The reality of just how close I had come to being immolated settled in and, rather than fear, I felt the boiling coil of a normally hidden rage somewhere deep in my stomach.

I threw my bag in the cab, slid in behind the wheel and shut the door, fumbling through the keys. It took a minute, but I found the right one, slammed it into the ignition, and brought the engine to life.

The window beside my head exploded inward, shards of safety glass peppering my already sliced-up cheek. A hand grabbed my shoulder, pulling me out of my seat. I thrashed on pure reflex, slapping and beating at the hand as it pulled me out through the window and dropped me, rather unceremoniously, to the ground.

I got a face full of dirt and gravel. On instinct, I started scrambling backwards. Cash stalked me, eyes locking on me in a death stare. He took two steps and kicked me in the side, hard, a whole new nucleus of pain erupting through my ribs, spears of pain shooting through my chest, every attempt at breathing causing me to choke out a gasp of agony. I tried crawling again. He kicked me again. This time he got my other side. The pain met in the middle, and for a moment it felt like my heart was going to stop and my lungs were collapsing.

I rolled onto my back, and Cash pounced, both hands wrapping around my throat. Instantly, the little air I was able to suck into my lungs was cut off completely. I started thrashing again, slamming my fists into his arms, swinging at his head, bucking my hips, trying everything I possibly could to throw him off of me.

The harder I fought, the tighter he squeezed. My head felt hot. A high-pitched ringing filled my ears. My vision, already off kilter from the light show, started to shrink down to pin points. I lost control over my ability to differentiate the two worlds, physical and spiritual, and saw threads of vivid colors trace their way through the little bit of sight I had left. My arms felt heavy. My hands went numb, falling into the dirt. I reached out blindly, fingertips feeling at the ground. My hand settled on something, a rough, jagged piece of quartz roughly the size of a softball, and in a last burst of adrenaline and willpower, I swung it upwards as hard as I was able—and connected.

Air filled my lungs, mouthfuls of glorious, cool, night

air. I coughed and sputtered, rolling onto my side. My skin tingled, like my whole body had gone to sleep. My vision returned, equal parts physical and spiritual. I could see the spirits of the forest, the trees thousands of times taller than they should have been. Animal spirits, silhouetted against the dark, watched from the treeline, eyes blazing in shades of yellow, red, and bright, bio-luminescent green. In the distance, howls, loud and undulating, shattered the silence. Beneath it all, the mundane world hung pale and shadowed, like a fading photograph. It took a moment, but my head cleared and I was able to put up the mental blocks I needed to shut out the spirit world. Cash was a few feet away from me, on his hands and knees, the side of his face painted with blood.

Cash and I both managed to work our way up to our knees. He was wobbly, swaying back and forth like he was drunk. For the first time in a long time, I wasn't the one that was worse for the wear.

Cash turned his eyes in my direction and just the sight of his face, after everything he'd done to me, to people I know, people I cared about, caused something in my brain to snap. Rage washed over me. This monster had tried to kill me. Not once, but twice. He'd tried to rape Melly. He'd threatened my father.

It wasn't going to happen again.

Everything went red.

I hit him again and this time, he dropped to his back. I leapt on top of him, swinging the quartz down, hard, against his temple. I felt him trying to push me away, weakly. I brushed his arms to the side and hit him again. The impact sounded like an egg dropping on the floor. It

registered somewhere far away, like an echo of an echo. I
hit him again and again.

When I finally stopped, my throat was raw. I had been
screaming. Tears were drying on my cheeks. I dropped the
rock and stared down at Cash. He was unrecognizable. His
face was a mass of blood and swollen flesh. His mouth was
open, though his lips were split and torn, teeth all broken.
One side of his head was misshapen.

Then reality came flooding back in.

"Cash?" I asked, shaking him.

He didn't answer.

"Cash?!" I asked again, my voice pitching upwards,
cracking. "Wake up you asshole! You don't…Cash…"

The understanding of what I'd done set in hard and
sudden, every bit as irrefutable as a universal truth. It was
a certainty that held the world down like gravity. I'd killed
him. I'd willfully taken another human being's life. I stood
up, took a few staggering steps backwards, horror and
revulsion hitting me in waves, and then fell backwards. I
had to fight to take my eyes off of Cash's body. I turned
and threw up, over and over again, emptying my stomach
on the side of some dirt road in the middle of nowhere. My
whole body was shaking, violent, chattering tremors that
started somewhere in the center of my body and radiated
outwards, towards my fingers.

My brain started processing the scenario in slow
motion, each thought weighed down with abject horror
and disgust, tempered with the realization of how this was
going to play out. If his brother knew where he was, or
what he was doing, and Cash didn't come back and I did,
well, the Carvers would do absolutely everything in their

power to kill me. What was left of them, that is. I couldn't call the cops. Most of them were on the Carvers' payroll, hated me, or both.

"Shit!" I yelled. "Shit, shit, shit!"

I had to get rid of the body. I had to put it somewhere where no one would find it. Then, I had to get away from here. A swell of emotion, more rage, fear, and disgust flooded over me.

I was already bleeding from the beating Cash had given me. I wiped blood off my face and onto my fingertips and drew the summoning sigil in the dirt.

CHAPTER 24

The earth elemental wasn't anything dramatic. It didn't have a face or a shape, or anything even remotely similar to features that would denote a personality. It looked like a pile of different types of rocks in all shapes and sizes, with a few fist-sized gemstones thrown into the mix for good measure. Though I couldn't tell you how, I was pretty sure it was looking at me.

Elementals, as it were, are some of the easier spirits to deal with, or summon for that matter. The sigil for an earth spirit is just a straight line with two dots over the top of it. Like any spirit, they have a personality archetype that tends to apply to most any of their ilk. Fire spirits are like hyper children. Air spirits have a memory and attention span like a goldfish. Water spirits are abhorrently moody. Earth spirits, on the other hand, are just lazy.

I heard the spirit's voice in my head, a sound comparable to pebbles rattling down a cliff face just before a coming avalanche, that my brain translated into words.

"What?" It asked.

"I need a favor."

"I'm not really in the mood to be charitable."

"What would put you in the mood," I asked, then added, "To be charitable, I mean."

"A nap."

"I need your help," I said, my voice trembling a bit.

"Yeah? I don't feel up to it," the elemental rumbled in the back of my head. "Better things to do."

"Seriously?"

"No, I'm lying. Yes, seriously. Can I go now?"

A small sliver of the rage I'd felt earlier slipped through.

"Open a hole, swallow that," I said, pointing to Cash's body.

"No."

"Last chance," I said.

"And what are you going to do?" it asked in a lazy drawl.

"I'll summon you back," I said.

"Oh, yeah, that's likely to change my mind."

"It won't. The crystal that I plan on binding you in might," I said, not mentioning that it would take me a month to purify it.

"You still won't get your hole," it said.

"Maybe not," I said. "Though I'm pretty sure I'll get a measure of satisfaction out of it."

The elemental fell silent. It suddenly felt weird that I was carrying on a conversation with a big pile of rocks. A moment later, Cash and the ground around him began to sink, the earth beneath him collapsing inwards, like a sinkhole. Within seconds, the hole was filled in. He was gone. It was like he'd never been there to begin with.

"Can I go now?" the elemental asked.

I reached out and broke the circle. It wasn't the kindest way to get rid of a spirit, since it basically sucked them back to the spirit world like they were a dust bunny in the path of an oncoming vacuum, but I wasn't really feeling that charitable myself.

Once the spirit was gone, I sat there, on my knees, staring at the spot where Cash had been. I knew what he'd done, what he'd tried to do, and I still felt something that I couldn't explain. There was an emptiness set in the middle of my chest. I looked down at my hands, stained with my blood, and more importantly, Cash's. His blood was literally on my hands.

The tears came in a torrent. I knew that I had irrevocably changed into something worse than I was, that I was completely and utterly different. Stained, for lack of a better word.

I finally stood, which in and of itself was a feat, and stumbled over to my truck. I grabbed the bottle of rum from my bag, opened it with my teeth, and turned the bottle towards the heavens. I didn't care that it burnt, that it turned my stomach with each swallow, I wanted it. No, I needed it. I needed it to fill that empty space in my gut.

I got a quarter of the way through the bottle before I grabbed my phone. I stared at it for a moment, my vision blurred, before I finally dialed Sam. He answered on the first ring. He's that kind of guy.

I didn't so much as say hello as let out a choked, aching sob.

"Jonah," he asked. "What's wrong?"

I didn't answer him. I couldn't, at least not yet. I just

sat there, making weak, tear-filled gasps and whines into the phone.

"Jonah, talk to me, what is it."

"I need help," I said, finally getting myself under some semblance of control.

"What is it? What happened?"

"I did something, Sam. I did something really bad."

"Jonah, what is it? You're not making any sense."

"Come get me," I said.

"Come get you? Where are you? What happened?"

"I don't know where I am. I just, I need help."

"Okay, okay. No problem. How do I find you?"

"My phone, find my phone," I said.

"Alright. I'm on my way," Sam said. "Stay put."

He hung up the phone. I sat down on the ground, next to my truck, bottle in one hand, phone still in the other. I wasn't sure how long I sat there, but when I saw headlights I was too drunk to be nervous. The bottle was on the ground beside me, empty for quite some time at this point. I was past the point of self-control, and I could see spirits drifting through the air, threads of power coursing through the ground, and a moon that far dwarfed the one most humans were accustomed to seeing. The headlights got closer, stopping a few feet behind my car. Sam appeared a moment later, in silhouette, rushing over towards me.

"Jonah," he said, then looked me over. "Jesus Christ, you're covered in blood. What the hell happened?"

I slurred something unintelligible.

Sam looked from me to the bottle, picked it up and shook his head.

"Should I assume this was full?"

"Mostly?" I said, which took a surprising amount of concentration to make coherent.

"I need to get you to a hospital. You've probably got alcohol poisoning at this point."

"No," I said, flailing weakly. "No."

"Jonah," Sam protested.

"No!" I yelled.

Sam sighed.

"Fine, alright. No hospital. C'mon, get up," he said, wedging an arm under my shoulder. At this point, nothing hurt. Despite being barely five feet and some change, Sam had muscle to spare. He lifted me up with minimal effort and led me to the back seat of his car, a newer model black Japanese sedan, and helped me in. After that everything started spinning and then I said "hello" to darkness, my old friend.

CHAPTER 25

When I woke up on the couch at Sam's gym I was in an absolutely bountiful smorgasbord of aches and pains. I'd managed to drink most of them away the night before, to the point that my newest miseries had subsided by the time Sam had picked me up. Now, they'd gotten together, planned an assault, and were in the process of mounting one hell of an offensive. My face stung from the stitches, a relatively minor inconvenience. Each breath felt tight and blossomed as a dull ache across my chest and back. My head hurt the most, a sharp, thudding pain that rested just behind my eyes. I was pretty sure I'd pulled more than a few muscles in my shoulder when I'd beaten...

No.

I was NOT going to think about that.

I wasn't sure what time it was, and there weren't any windows to speak of. My internal clock said it was morning, maybe noon, but there was no telling. I heard music.

Michael Jackson, actually. "Billie Jean," no, "Smooth Criminal." It was turned down low.

When I opened my eyes, which took way more effort than I'd expected, given the hangover I'd acquired, I realized two things. First, I was under about six blankets, the weight of which threatened to crush me. Second, Sam was sitting across from me on the small stools he usually kept near the corners of the boxing ring. He looked tired, his face drawn, concern tugging at his features.

"Morning sunshine," he said, grabbing a water bottle off the floor and passing it to me.

I didn't bother sitting up. I didn't think I could. I opened the bottle weakly, and took a sip. The water was pure liquid nirvana, cool, clean. It washed away the dryness that, until now, I hadn't even realized had coated my mouth and throat.

"Thanks," I said.

"Yep," Sam said, taking a slow breath, seeming to steel himself. "You were in some sad shape, Jonah."

"Judging by how I feel, I can only imagine."

"You want to tell me why I picked you up in the middle of nowhere, pissing on yourself drunk and covered in blood?"

"I couldn't have been that bad," I mumbled.

"No. You literally pissed on yourself. You were that bad," Sam stated, as matter of fact. "Then you threw up in the back of my car."

"Ouch. Sorry," I said.

"Six times. I seriously debated taking you to the hospital. Every time I mentioned it, you managed to gain enough clarity to call me an asshole and tell me, and I quote, 'Fuck you, you fucking fuck stick. I'm not going to any goddamn hospital. Take me and *I'll piss on your cat.*'"

"You don't even own a cat," I said.

"I'm aware."

"I, uh. Wow. I really am sorry."

"Yeah, you're going to be. You called me during date night."

I winced.

"Andy's fit to kill the both of us. I can't say I blame him," Sam continued.

"Well, that's just stellar."

"No, it's really not," Sam said, matter of fact. "I changed your dressings, wrapped up your ribs. A few are probably broken. I'm gonna stand by my recommendation of a hospital."

"Yeah, I'll pass."

"So what happened?"

I closed my eyes, turning my head away from Sam. I didn't want to talk about it. I knew I owed him an explanation, but just thinking about what I'd done sent my stomach wheeling towards an already perilous tipping point and woke up that same empty, stained feeling.

"I don't want to talk about it," I said, finally, my voice barely a whisper.

I shook my head, fighting back tears. After a moment, I sat up. This, of course, ignited a whole new plethora of discomforts, from new and exciting aches and pains to a roiling, cold nausea.

"Sam. I'd like to talk to my boy, if that's alright," came a voice from the far end of the room.

"Yeah, sure," Sam said and stood, walking to get his coat off one of the corner posts of the boxing ring.

I turned and saw my father. Behind him, Melly sat on the edge of the ring.

"I appreciate you picking him up and I'm sorry about your car," my father said.

"Nothing to be sorry about. That's what friends do," Sam said, throwing his jacket on. "Mind helping me get his truck?" he asked Melly.

"Not like I have anything better to do," she said. The two of them both turned, heading out.

My father sat down on the stool across from me and for a long time, just stared at me. I couldn't read what he was thinking, but the way he looked at me, the mixture of sadness, of desperation, and of love, made me feel like I was a kid again, when I couldn't stop repeating the lines I'd heard on a TV show, using them like some kind of mantra to keep myself focused under the onslaught of seeing two worlds simultaneously. It was the look he gave me when he knew it wasn't me making me do the things I did, it was something else, something outside of my control.

"What are you doing here," I asked, finally breaking the silence.

"Sam called me. Told me you were in a bad sort."

"I'm alright," I lied.

"Piss drunk, covered in blood, puking and pissing all over yourself? Sounds to me like a far cry from alright, Jonah."

"Pop—"

"Don't *Pop* me, Jonah. You're in some shit. That much is obvious," my old man said, his voice calm and even.

"I can handle it."

"Yeah? That why I have to play babysitter for that poor girl out there? Why I had to stitch you up after almost shooting one of Hank Carver's sons in my kitchen?"

"What happened to her isn't my fault," I said.

"Yeah? But she called you, you got involved. How'd you meet her, Jonah? She's the bartender at the Carvers' bar, ain't she? That says to me at the very least, you been going down there enough to make pals. Judging from the shape you're in most of the time when I see you, if I see you nowadays, you're frequenting that establishment at least semi-regular. I'm guessing a handful of others, too."

"Not this again," I said.

"Was I done talking?" my father asked. This time the dam broke and the emotion that came through was pure frustration.

"No," I said, petulant.

"That's what I thought. Now, thing is, most folks don't go to the Poor Confederate because they want to tie one on. They go because they're into no good. So, you want to tell me what kind of trouble you're in?"

"Look—" I started to say.

He cut me off.

"The next words out of your mouth better be truth, or I'm going to barbecue your ass in molasses, you hear me?"

I opened my mouth to say something.

"Don't you lie to me, Jonah. Don't. I'm not playing around with you on this."

I sighed, deflated.

"Your mother, after your sister passed, she kept secrets.

She kept secrets right up until she left. I ain't gonna let you drown in that too, you understand me? Now, start talking."

I closed my eyes, trying to think past the thudding inside my skull. I honestly believed my father wanted to help. That he'd do whatever it was in his power that he could to help me. I just wasn't sure I could tell him something like this. I wasn't sure I could handle the look of disappointment, of disgust. Of all people in the world, it was his disapproval I couldn't bear. I was already a disappointment, I knew that much. If I told him, I was going far past the point of no return. Then again, if I didn't, I would be, in a lot of ways, like my mother. I would be abandoning him the same way she had after my sister's suicide.

"I did something bad, Pop," I said, finally.

"Alright?"

"No, real bad."

"So, enough with the prelude. Just tell me."

The tears came again, harder this time. Within seconds, any semblance of restrained emotion was gone, and I was doubled over, my hands over my face. My father sat down on the couch next to me and put a hand on my shoulder. That was enough, that one gesture, as simple as it was, spoke more in that moment than any words he could've said to me.

"I killed him. I killed that son of a bitch," I admitted. "I killed him, Pop. I had to. He was going to set me on fire. Hurt you, Melly. I had to."

"Wait, what?"

"I had to do it, Pop."

My father shook his head, trying to take in what I was saying.

"Slow down. Tell me what happened."

I laid the whole story out for him, at least the parts he needed to hear. I started all the way at the beginning, with the money I'd borrowed from the Carvers to fix his shop. I told him about the parking lot and the beating they'd given me. I told him how, after we'd argued on the porch, I'd left and Cash had jumped me outside my house and drug me out to a field with the intention of turning me into a briquette. I told him about killing Cash and burying him under a dirt road out in the middle of nowhere.

When I'd finished, my father squeezed my shoulder again, then stood. He paced back and forth for a few minutes while I sat there, tears drying on my cheek. I didn't feel any better. I didn't feel any worse. I just felt that I'd become something different, something I wasn't wholly okay with in the slightest.

"Damn it, Jonah," he said. "Damn it. Damn it, damn it, damn it."

"Pop, I—"

My father stood up, running his hands through his hair and started walking. He'd go a few steps then turn, pacing back and forth while his brain worked. I'd seen him do this a million times. Usually when I screwed things up. I'd learned a long time ago it was best to let my old man pace and keep my mouth shut until he settled down. After a few minutes, he seemed to deflate, the anger draining out of him.

"Pop?" I asked finally, after watching him pace.

"You did what you had to do," he said finally, "You didn't have a choice." My father's voice held a weary resignation that I'd never heard before. It sounded like he was trying to convince himself every bit as much as he was trying to convince me. "I don't like it. I get it, but... damn, son. The Carvers aren't going to take this light in the slightest."

I hadn't really been expecting that. When he sat down on the couch beside me, he did it with a stare so intense that it brokered no room for argument or comment.

"Listen to me, and listen good. This is the last you speak of this; you understand me?"

"Uh, I—"

"Do. You. Understand?" he asked, enunciating each word sharply. "Never a word."

"Yes, I get it."

"Good. Now, here's what's going to happen. I'm gonna go talk to Hank Carver and get you time to get this straight. I don't care how you do it, but you fix this mess. Anyone asks you, you ain't seen that Carver boy since he was at our house. That's a mess we can't clean up. There's going to be hell to pay. Maybe we'll get lucky and they won't put the two and two together to get Jonah."

"I get it," I said.

"I don't think you do, but that's not important. Once you get ahead of this, I want you to pack a bag."

"What?"

"Pack a bag, because I'm slapping your ass in rehab."

"You're what?" I asked.

"You heard me. I'm putting you in rehab. God knows you need it, and this will get you off the Carvers' radar until I clean this damned mess up."

"That's ridiculous. I don't need rehab."

"Yeah? Let me ask you something? You think Gretchen

were to see you like this, she'd be happy with what she saw?" my father asked, and instantly I felt barely more than a few inches tall. The whole reason my father was here, alive and reaming me a new one, was because of Gretchen. Shamans, by their nature, were healers. My father had had lung cancer. He hadn't known it at the time. She took it from him, pulled it into herself and saved him. A few months later, I was holding her hand when, after chemo, losing part of a lung, she just couldn't fight anymore.

I opened my mouth to say something and my father gave me a look that set my blood frigid.

"Try and argue with me," he said, finally. "Tell me I'm wrong."

I knew that there wasn't any argument I could wage that would end up with me being the victor of this situation. A part of me also knew he wasn't wrong.

Outside, I heard the familiar rumble of my truck. My father didn't say a word. He simply stood, and marched off towards the door, throwing it open. Sam came in a second later, followed by Melly. Sam cast a glance over his shoulder as my father passed and then tossed me my keys. They hit me in the chest and fell on the floor.

"I taped some plastic over the window."

I stood, albeit weakly, and realized I was wearing a pair of Sam's pajama pants. They were too small, too tight, red, covered with little palm trees, and left a good four inches of my calves exposed.

"Your old man brought a change of clothes. I'll get them for you. Your phone was dead, it's on the charger in your truck," Sam said. "I think you have a cane somewhere around here, too."

CHAPTER 26

I said my goodbyes to Sam and Melly, my mind wrestling with everything my father said as I walked outside to my truck. He was right, of course, getting me out of here for a little while would put me out of mind. Maybe the Carvers would forget about me, at least enough that they wouldn't come asking questions about Cash. Still, I'd seen my father put down his fair share of the sauce, and he wanted me to go to rehab. It wasn't fair and it sure as hell wasn't his call, nor his place to start passing that kind of judgment.

Sam had taped clear plastic over the window Cash shattered, which was kind enough. It would keep the wind and the rain out, but I couldn't see a damn thing through it. I checked under the seat and found my bag where I'd left it, everything still intact. I scooped my phone up off the seat, disconnected it from the spiraled cord and turned it on. I grabbed a few sips from my emergency flask in the glovebox while I waited for the fun dancing logos, the main screen popped up…along with seventeen voice mails.

Every last one of them from Lysone, save for one from Gus. I listened to that one first.

It was two seconds of silence, then a click. Given Gus's paranoid nature and his refusal to speak to answering machines because some shadowy shadow government within a shadowy shadow government would compile voice profiles, I took that as a message to call him back. The phone rang once, then clicked, then rang again with a completely different tone, then clicked, repeat, click, repeat. Finally, Gus answered.

"Jonah?" he said by way of greeting.

"Gus."

"So, I have some very good news," he said.

"Oh, thank god," I muttered.

"I managed to sell your books."

"How much?" I asked.

"Well, we could go to Vegas and have a hell of a time."

"That would involve you leaving the house for more than thirty seconds, which you haven't done since—"

"Nineteen eighty-four. Orwell was right, you know?"

"Right, how much?"

"Minus my fee, we're looking at around ninety-five hundred."

"Seriously?"

"Yep, someone wanted that old diary pretty bad. Fetched a nice chunk of change."

"Well, that's a plus," I said, starting the truck. That, coupled with whatever I could hustle Lysone for, would leave me out of the Carvers' debt and, quite possibly, carrying a few extra bucks in my pocket.

"You alright? You sound rough," Gus asked.

"Bad night. Listen, Gus, do you have enough money on you that you can float me until everything clears?"

"I have it in gold. I don't trust paper money."

"Wait. What?" I asked.

"I don't trust paper money. Those strips they put in it? They're data recorders," he said. "They take samples of touch DNA, record fingerprints."

"Right. Gold's fine," I said. "Mind if I swing by tonight?"

"I don't have any plans. I may stream a Tori Spelling documentary, if that interests you?"

"I, no, no it doesn't. Not at all."

"You sure?" he asked.

"Positive."

"Ah well. Thought I'd offer," he said.

"Much obliged," I said. "See you in a few hours?"

"Sounds like a plan," Gus said.

I hung up the phone and started the truck, backing out of the small lot that sat behind Sam's gym. The phone rang again when I pulled out into traffic. I didn't bother reading the name. I just answered it.

"Hello," I said.

"Mister Heywood."

"Miss Lysone."

"I take it there is a good reason why you never arrived to our meeting?"

I cut a quick glance to myself in the mirror. My bandages were clean, but my face underneath was a myriad of bruises, scrapes, and cuts.

"You could say that," I said.

"I see. Is the fragment still safe?" she asked, and

once again her voice was colored with the slightest bit of desperation.

"As houses."

She sighed with relief. All in all, Lysone still threw me off. There was something about the way she'd been so cool and detached, so in control in the beginning. Yet now, the closer she got to that damned rock, the more she seemed to need it. She sounded like an addict getting closer to a fix. It freaked me out, just a little. It also told me I had a damned good chance of managing to pull more money out of her if I played my cards right.

"Do you think you can work me into your schedule now?" she asked, a slight edge coming back to her voice, that control in tone reasserting itself.

"Well, that depends."

"Pardon?"

"I said that depends."

"On?" she asked.

"On how the next few minutes of this conversation proceed," I said.

"I take it you have some sort of proposal," she said, making no effort to hide the fact that she was patronizing me.

"Actually, yes. See, I did a little research on this rock. It's a bona fide hunk of the Ledberg Runestone, you'll be happy to know. It's also got some juice to it, and I'm pretty sure you follow my meaning."

"It is and I do, yet I fail to see how this is relevant to our previously held arrangement."

"Because the terms of our previous arrangement are in need of a little alteration," I said. I'd been letting the tide carry me for too long. It was time I started taking a little bit of control and start swimming. To be honest, it felt good to be playing the game, to be the one doing the hustling and not the one getting hustled.

"Is that so?"

"It is. See, the way I figure it, this rock is worth easily fifty, sixty thousand to the right person. Initially, you were going to offer me twenty thousand, then it dropped down to five. I'm feeling generous, so how about ten thousand and we call it a day?"

There was a long stretch of silence. I drove mostly up and down side streets, circling back on myself, wasting time while I waited for her to talk.

"And if I refuse?"

"Well, at the moment I'm going roughly eighty miles an hour down Interstate forty," I lied. "Think maybe this rock would hold up if I drop it out a window? Hell, I could probably find another buyer if need be."

"I think you couldn't possibly be that stupid," she said.

"You'd be amazed how stupid I can be," I said, and instantly regretted it.

"Perhaps not."

"So, what's it going to be? Do I drop it out the window? Find another buyer? Or do we come to an agreement?"

"Do you know how quickly I could kill you, if I so chose?" Lysone asked. She delivered that news the same way Cash would: emotionless, flat, like it was just an item on a to-do list. The thought of Cash set my stomach to rolling. I didn't answer for a second, opting to take a deep breath and compose myself.

The fact that she was willing to kill for it, assuming she was telling the truth, told me that I'd gotten to her. That she believed I had what she was after. I didn't doubt she could kill me if she wanted to, but for now, I had the advantage.

"Supposing you could, that seems a bit like overkill," I said. "There's also no guarantee that if you did that, I'd have it on me when you did. Seems an awful lot of work on a guess. Ten grand, that's it. Less than you offered the first time, more than the second. I think it's perfectly reasonable. Besides, the offer is time limited. You either take it or I start looking at other options. I can meet you now, and we can both walk away happy."

"As much as it pains me, I suppose you have a point."

"So, Jack of the Wood then? Say half an hour?"

"It would seem so," she said.

"Good," I said, pulling into the same lot that Waylon and his brother had seen fit to beat the bejesus out of me in, two doors down from Jack of the Wood. I sat in my truck, staring at the walls, at the traffic. My hands were shaking and I was coated in sweat when I finally got out. I grabbed my bag, complete with the rock, tossed it over my shoulder, and walked inside my favorite bar.

CHAPTER 27

One of the many reasons I love Jack of the Wood is the music. Tonight's fare was a band belting out traditional Irish tunes. A decent crowd had shown up for the festivities, and there was the chatter of bar patrons, the clatter of glasses and bottles, all mixing with the fiddle and acoustic guitar of the band. The joint had a lot of history. It was the kind of place where stories were shared over glasses and a whole hell of a lot of merry got made.

I got my drink at the bar, a double of one of their better Irish whiskeys, and scanned the crowd. I knew a lot of the faces, some of them by name. A few glasses got raised in my direction. I ignored them, trying to pick Lysone out of the crowd.

When I finally spotted her, it was in a booth at the back. People seemed to avoid her, walking out and away from her table rather than going straight past her. I wrote it off as a vibe she gave off. After all, she wasn't exactly the most friendly or inviting woman I'd ever met.

Attractive, yes. "Inviting" wasn't a word I'd associate with her. A glass of water sat in front of her, the outside thick with condensation.

It took me more than a minute to wade through the crowd, which was heavy with college kids interspersed with the regulars. The band drifted from one upbeat drinking song to another, the patrons with them in force, slurring along to every verse. I slid into the booth across from Lysone. Her eyes snapped towards me. There was desperation in them, something that I hadn't seen the other times we'd spoken. There was something else, too. Something dark and primal that I couldn't really put my finger on. It wasn't so much her body language. It was more of an aura, which I guess explained why people were choosing to avoid her. Hell, I wanted to avoid her at this particular moment, and I was about to make a decent sum of money off of her.

"You have it?" she asked, a sharp edge to her tone.

"I do."

"Give it to me," she said.

"No," I said.

She blinked, a look on her face like she'd been slapped. "No?"

"No."

Lysone stared at me, her eyes narrowed. Finally, she settled back in the booth, arms crossing over her chest, a slight tug of a smirk at her lips.

"Ah, I see now," she said.

I threw an arm casually across the back of the booth. For almost the span of an entire song, we sat like that, staring at each other. I broke first, wiping sweat from forehead with the back of my hand. A small smile tugged at Lysone's lips. She was like a hungry wolf catching the scent of a very tiny, very scared bunny.

"This is, I believe you call it, the hustle, correct?"

I shrugged.

"Actually no hustle whatsoever. It's pretty cut and dry."

"Ah," she said with a patronizing smile. "By all means, carry on."

I'd be lying if I said that her reaction was doing wonders to bolster my confidence regarding this transaction. Either way, I was all in, I had to play it out to the end whichever way it went.

"The price has gone up. It's that simple," I said, trying to exude as much confidence as I possibly could.

"Has it?"

"It has," I said, matter of fact. "See, I did a little digging. It turns out your magic pebble is worth quite a bit to the right buyer. Matter of fact, it's worth quite a bit more than your initial offer. So, we're going to renegotiate," I said. Even to my own ears, I didn't sound entirely sure of myself. Hell, I was starting to think I sounded more like a scared middle schooler asking a girl to a first dance than I did a con artist, practitioner and channeler of primordial mystical forces, or spell-slinging master of the occult arts.

Lysone quirked a brow and nodded for me to continue.

"Ten thousand. Cash."

"Ten thousand dollars in cash?" Lysone asked, though she sounded more amused than inquisitive. I was hoping for at least resigned, maybe insulted. This was not going as planned.

I narrowed my eyes, trying to get a read on her. There was something underneath her facade, something that I couldn't quite put a name to. It was dark and violent. The reality of how out of my depth I was had started to creep in at the edges of my nerves and it was taking a ton of willpower to not get up and run.

"There's another option," Lysone said, pitching her voice to something just above a whisper.

"No, there isn't," I said, keeping as much bravado in my voice as I could.

"But there is."

"Fine," I said with a shrug, trying to appear nonchalant. "There's other people that will pay me for this. I came to you first, since you're the one that made the initial job offer. Call it courtesy."

"A courtesy? You tried to shake me down."

"Nature of the game. Don't like it? Don't play," I said.

Lysone settled back in her booth and took a small sip of water. She set the glass back on the table and traced one fingertip through a small droplet of water.

"Mister Heywood, let me spell something out for you," Lysone said, turning her eyes back towards me. Her voice had changed. Before, it had just been icy. Now, each and every word seemed to reverberate with power. The very air around Lysone felt cold, oppressive. It reminded me of the few hours just before a blizzard, when it feels like the entire world has changed, becoming something desolate and heavy with the impending wrath of Mother Nature. I'd felt power before, but Lysone had just changed the game. Everything around us had become quiet, not because they had stopped talking, but because just sitting near Lysone had blocked out the sound.

Whatever she'd done to conceal what she was, she'd

just taken that camouflage off, and I was in the presence of a power far older, far stronger, and far more callous than anything I'd ever experienced in my life. My hindbrain, that part that focuses on survival, was going into convulsions, dumping me with adrenaline and a resounding need to run. My whole body was shaking. I felt hot and cold at the same time, like my body didn't know how to react to being near Lysone anymore.

"You are, as the saying goes, out of your league. You are a very, very small cog in a very big machine. I could kill you and everyone in this room, with nothing more than a thought," she smiled slowly, a predator's smile. "To be perfectly honest, I could wipe this insignificant pin prick of a hall from the face of the map and spend less energy doing it than it takes you to blink."

I didn't say anything. Instead, I sat there, mouth open and precariously close to losing control of my bladder.

Lysone let the words hang in the air, then reached into her pocket and put an envelope on the table. She slid it towards me. Sound came rushing back in, the sound of the band, of the crowd, yet it was all sort of surreal and hard to take in. Things had changed in that moment. People, we like to think we're at the top of the food chain, the apex predators. Myself, everyone around me, we were insignificant compared to Lysone, whoever or whatever she was.

"Now, what you owe me. I want it," Lysone said, taking a very girlish and demure sip from her glass. "Put it on the table."

My heart, still thudding at roughly the pace of a speed metal drumline, drowned out the words.

Lysone tapped one nail against the table, the sound

so sharp in the din of noise that it hit me like a slap in the face.

"The stone. On the table," she said. "Go on, you can do it."

I reached into my bag, my hand trembling, and withdrew the stone. Almost instantly that feeling of its power washed over me. Only now, there was malevolence in it. It was like the stone itself wanted to be near Lysone. It practically hummed with metaphysical bad intent.

I set it on the table and immediately regretted it. I should have never even brought the damned thing to her. I should have never taken this little heist-for-hire on to begin with. But I had, and now because I had, something terrible was going to happen. I wasn't sure what, exactly, but I knew it like I knew that Han shot first and that there was a special spot in hell reserved for the jackass who cancelled Firefly.

As soon as my hand left the hides wrapped around the stone, a nearly cosmic weight settled onto my shoulders. I suddenly understood what Pontius Pilate had felt like when he'd washed his hands. Worse yet, I had absolutely no idea why.

Lysone gave me a brief nod of thanks, a wink, and just like that, she vanished. The stone was gone, she was gone, and I was left sitting there still shaking, scared out of my mind, and feeling like the biggest mark on the planet.

I sat in Jack of the Wood for a long, long time. Hours at least. I didn't drink. I didn't even move. The last vestiges of Lysone's power had faded only seconds after she'd vanished.

While I sat there I tried to reconnect to humanity. It sounds odd, but I needed the feeling that came with being near other living, breathing humans. After getting just the slightest taste of whatever that woman, or woman-shaped thing, was, I needed the reassurance. I was scared to leave. You hear stories about monsters, about things that we can't explain, but to be in the presence of that much sheer power was something wholly and entirely different.

When I finally left, the night had turned ominous, heavy. In the distance I could see an illuminated cross outside of a church, one of its light bulbs burnt out. The light it threw off only made the shadows seem longer and darker.

I'd left my phone in the truck, and the little screen displayed two missed calls. One from Sam and one from Gus. It was already pushing past midnight, so I figured all the trouble I'd gotten Sam in, I could wait until the next day to call him back. The last thing I needed was for Andy to start throwing a fit thinking Sam had some strange man calling him in the middle of the night.

I called Gus back, and the phone didn't even ring. Not much of a surprise there, but with no other place I could think of to go at the moment, and the debt with the Carvers still hanging over my head, I pointed my truck in that direction and started driving.

CHAPTER 28

When I got to Gus's, the gate was laying in the driveway, torn off its hinges. The security camera, usually mounted on a long metal pole, lay next to it on the ground.

I didn't get out of my truck. Instead, I turned into the driveway and made the short half-mile trek in record speed.

The front of the house told the same story, the front door had been torn off and now lay at the bottom of the steps. A few of the yard gnomes had been relocated to the front yard, hard enough that they were in pieces. I saw wires sticking out of some of the gnomish debris.

I killed the engine and sat in my truck, listening to the motor tick. Everything was silent. This far out, there should have been the song of cicadas, an owl, bullfrog, something.

I got out of the truck, leaning on my cane for support, and stood there. Waiting, hoping to hear something. Anything.

Nothing came.

It took me a few minutes for me to muster up the nerve,

but I finally made my way to the stairs. I moved slowly, not just because of the cane, or the fear of what was waiting in the wings. There was no telling what sort of traps Gus had set up. For all I knew, I'd take two steps and end up in a pungie pit, or a bear trap, or hell, both at once.

I could smell something ticky, metallic, and heavy before I even crossed the threshold.

Blood. Lots of it.

I saw Gus after I made it a few steps into the living room. He was on his knees in a puddle of blood roughly as wide across as I was tall. He was trussed up, bound at the wrists. I couldn't see his face, but his back had been laid open to the point that his ribs had been severed, separated from his spine. In the gloom, the bones were almost glowing.

"Oh, Christ Gus," I said quietly, closing my eyes and leaning against one of the exposed studs.

It took everything I had to look at the room again, to open my eyes and once more take in the scene of my friend's death. I wanted to run out of there, to turn tail and bolt. I wanted to scream. I wanted to blink and for all of this to be gone.

It wasn't.

I took a slow step towards Gus, careful to keep my cane out of the pooling blood.

When he took a long, wheezing gasp, I let out something between a squeak and a full-blown shriek.

I rushed to him, caught in a rush of adrenaline. I knelt in front of him.

His eyes were glazed, but focused. His face drawn and pale. It took him a moment, but he lifted his head and met my eyes.

"Jonah," he wheezed.

"Don't talk, Gus. Let me get you down," I said.

I looked towards his wrists, with the intention of cutting his binds. The problem with that plan, though, was there was nothing binding him. His arms were stretched out, to the point it looked like they were about to be pulled out of their sockets, but there was nothing holding him.

A spell. He was being held by a spell.

I could work with this. As long as I could figure out what the spell was, I could get him down. I just needed to think. After Lysone, and especially after Cash, I needed a win and this was my chance to put one on the boards.

"Hang in there, brother. Let me get you down."

I stood up and took a step back from Gus, and began to let the mental walls in my mind slip away. The spirit world slowly slipped into focus.

The interior of Gus's house didn't look any different, physically speaking. There were still the same exposed beams and walls, the same strings of photos all tied up in a big conspiracy-tracing web. Slowly, however, other things came into view.

A green glow began to emanate from everything, seeping through the beams, the floor, the ceilings, a psychic echo of my friend's special blend of insanity. Fear spirits, shadows that shifted and morphed from screaming faces to all varying manner of insects, scuttled over the floors, the ceiling, crawling over each other and every exposed surface in the room.

There were chains around Gus's wrists, binding him to two of the beams in his living room. It was a simple spell, a binding, the chains made solely out of energy and intent.

I could negate them with next to no effort. Someone like Gus, on the other hand, with no magical talent whatsoever, would be held for as long as the spell remained present.

Then I saw the woman, standing at the far side of the room. She was tall. Her hair was blonde, worked into elaborate braids, which, aside from looking cool, kept her long tresses out of her face. She wore a blue tunic-style shirt, which hung almost to her knees and pants made out of some form of skin, tucked into knee-high, fur boots. A gray cloak was wrapped around her shoulders. She was leaning on a spear, the handle made of some dark, polished wood, the head made of what looked like iron.

I knew instantly what she was and what she was here for. I'd met her ilk before, once. They appeared right at that moment of a person's death. They were amongst the most powerful spirits in the spiritual pecking order, just below angels and demons and a step or two away from gods. They were known to everyone, at least once in their life, and in most cases feared simply because of what they were. Everyone believed in, and was, on some level, scared of Death. Though, in their defense, death spirits were mind-numbingly neutral, single-minded, and mostly didn't give a rat's ass about us outside of their work.

I fought back tears. I couldn't do anything to help my friend. That time had come and gone, everything from here on out, for Gus, was inevitable.

The woman and I stared at each other for a long moment. I didn't move.

Finally, she looked from me, to the chains. Her eyes fell back on me again and she nodded, just once.

I got a stick of sage and a pocketknife out of my bag.

I stuck the sage under my arm and used the knife to cut a small line across my palm. In the spirit world, my blood, with its inherent magic properties, was a vibrant red. I smeared the blood across the sage, pocketed the knife, and withdrew a lighter. The blood, once mixed with the energies held in the sage, cause the whole smudge stick to light up like a torch in the spirit world. I lit the sage, and the blood, and let the smoke drift over the chains, focusing my intent. It took less than a second for the magic to take hold and the smoke, where it hit the chains, dissolved them as quickly as if I'd doused them in acid.

I caught Gus and lowered him to the floor, which, given his size, was damn near hernia inducing.

"I didn't scream, brother," Gus said, barely able to choke out a whisper. "She didn't make me scream."

"I know, Gus, you did good."

"Bitch," he muttered.

"Who was it?" I asked.

Gus nodded towards his computers.

"Cameras, I got her on camera. They finally got me, Jonah. I told you they would. I knew too much."

"You just rest, Gustonian. Relax. I'm gonna call for some help. They'll get you fixed up," I said. I knew it was lie. So did he.

Gus coughed, his head lolling around. What little strength he had left was rapidly fading.

"Top drawer, my desk," he said.

"What?"

Gus shook his head.

"Be easy, brother," Gus said.

In the span of a blink, Gus was standing behind his

body. The Valkyrie stood behind him. Gus looked at me, then his body, and smiled. There was none of the jittery, paranoid sort of energy that seemed to constantly radiate around him in life. Instead, he seemed calm. The Valkyrie put a hand on his shoulder and they both faded away, leaving me on the floor, holding the rapidly cooling body of one of my best friends in a pool of his own blood.

CHAPTER 29

I sat like that for a long time, saying my silent goodbyes to my friend. Finally, I lay him as gently as I could on the floor and stood, walking over to his computer. I had absolutely no idea how to do much of anything with it, let alone track down the footage of whoever it was that had killed him.

So I did what any rational, technologically challenged spell-slinger would do in just such a situation. I started pushing buttons at random.

Apparently, that was only a half bad idea. Screens started flashing. Somewhere in the distance, Phil Collins starting belting out "Sussudio," a few lights flickered, and something that sounded like a large machine started up in the basement. A small window popped up on one of the screens, the picture grainy, jittering back and forth for a second with interference, but gradually becoming clear enough that I could see who was standing at Gus's gate.

Lysone. Judging from the time stamp, she had been

here at roughly the same time I'd been sitting in my truck outside of Jack of the Wood.

It was the exact same time Gus had been calling me and I hadn't bothered to pick up the phone.

I hit the spacebar and the video clip started playing. There was no sound, and the picture quality wasn't up to snuff, but it was clear enough.

Lysone held one hand out, and the camera went to static for only an instant. When the picture resumed, she was stepping over the fallen gate, the camera starting to lean and fall. Then, it went dark.

I wasn't sure how I should feel. On the one hand, I was nearly consumed with anger and grief. My friend had been murdered in cold blood, I could only assume because he had been trying to help me decipher the stone, which I didn't even have anymore.

On the other hand, I was terrified. I'd seen, at least in part, Lysone for what she truly was, and it wasn't even close to human. She was so far above my pay grade that it wouldn't take much for her to squash me like a bug if I went after her for revenge. Not to mention I felt like about ten miles of bad road. I was nauseous and pouring sweat, my hands were shaking, and I quite possibly had a fever of some sort.

Last, but not least, I was lost. I'd tried playing the hero before, and I'd failed. All I got was this lousy cane and a month in intensive care. I didn't know what Lysone truly was. I didn't know what the stone could really do. I didn't know if it even mattered. Lysone claimed she wanted to retrieve it because it had belonged to her husband. Having felt the power that radiated out of it and seen how badly she needed it, I didn't buy that for a second. Though, even with that in mind, I had no idea what she could or would do with it if she chose to tap into its power.

The longer I stood there, slack-jawed and staring at the monitors, the less sure I became of anything.

I reached down and opened the top drawer of Gus's desk, almost without thinking. There were two bags filled with gold jewelry. Judging from the heft of the sacks, it was way more than I'd needed. He'd known I was in a situation.

Gus had come through once again.

"So how does this story play out now?" a voice asked from behind me.

I turned, all but jumping out of my skin in the process.

The girl from the parking lot, the girl who'd killed Mama Duvalier's daughter, stood a few feet away. She had a man with her, if you can technically call someone as large as the individual behind her, a man. He was well over seven feet tall, standing hunched over in Gus's living room. I was pretty sure that his shoulders were wide enough to equal roughly two of me, and not a single bit of his physique looked like it was composed of fat. His clothing was simple: jeans and a white t-shirt. He wore his hair long, almost to the middle of his back, accentuated here and there with braids. His beard, which hung almost to the middle of his chest, was decorated the same way, only the braids were covered with tiny silver beads. He had two black eyes.

I was a little slow on the uptake, but I finally recognized him. It was the same guy that had attacked me at Abandon and had played defensive lineman with my truck.

"Damn it," I muttered, taking a step back and bumping into Gus's desk.

"You look frightened," the girl said.

"Well, you're nuts and he tried to kill me," I said. "Actually, you're both killers."

"And you aren't?" the girl asked me. I glared.

"Did you try to kill him, Canute?"

The girl looked at her companion, quirking one thin brow. Canute didn't say anything.

"Well, Canute, is this true?"

"Of course not."

"You threw me across a parking lot, tried to stomp on my head, and then almost crashed my car," I said.

"I was trying to stop you, not kill you."

"By breaking my freaking neck?"

"You'd have stopped, wouldn't you?"

I stared at him for a long moment. I hated it when the, well, whoever the hell he was, had a point. He didn't look away. I did.

The girl watched this exchange, her head snapping back and forth like a tennis spectator. When we'd finished talking, she nodded her head once, obviously satisfied that whatever quarrel there was, was successfully at its end.

"There's a lot of illr around you."

"A lot of what?"

She ignored me.

"He's a coward," Canute said, finally. "I don't understand your interest."

"That makes two of us," I said.

The girl turned towards me, tilting her head ever so slightly. She took two steps forward. I tried to take two steps back, and found myself sitting on Gus's keyboard.

"Sussudio" cued up again. Canute looked around, confused at the sudden sonic intrusion.

The girl looked over at Gus's body, then back towards me.

"We should prepare the pyre for your friend," she said, walking past me.

• • •

We stood there, for hours, watching the fire consume Gus. The girl, whatever her name was, and Canute stood on either side of me, watching the flames reach higher into the night sky. None of us said anything. We just watched him go. When the flames had finally dissipated, Canute took the body, vanishing into the woods around Gus's home.

A small glimmer caught my eye, laying at the foot of the pyre. I walked over, kicking around with my toe. A small piece of metal, cut into the shape of an ax head lie on the ground, its surface engraved with knot work. A leather cord ran through it. I reached down, scooping it off the grass and held it in my hand, then slid it into my pocket. It had been Gus's. I'd never seen him wear it, but I could all but feel that twitchy sort of vibe of his radiating off it.

"Do you have a name?" I asked the girl, finally.

"I have a name."

"Care to share?"

"You're allowed to call me Kari."

"Kari, huh?" I nodded. "Tell me something, Kari."

"The average worth of a human body broken down into its chemical components is roughly one dollar and seventy-three cents."

"I," I sighed. "Not what I meant."

Kari turned to look at me. She still had that same aura of power, almost on par with Lysone's but wholly different. Whereas Lysone's had felt predatory, Kari's was sort of inevitable. It was something constant, but subtle, like the tides. It was surprising to see radiating off a girl who looked like a teenage groupie for Skid Row.

"Oh," she said. "What do you want me to tell you?"

"The stone, what does it do?"

"Horrible things. She has two of the pieces she needs. The stone and the blood of a godborn."

"So it's a spell?"

"Of sorts."

"Right, okay. How bad."

"Very."

"Can you be less vague?"

"I could," she said, putting a hand on my shoulder and turning me to face her. Her other hand rose to my temple, absently brushing away a few strands of hair. I felt the steady ebb of her power, her essence, radiating off of that touch. "You should know this, however. She considers you a threat. She'll come for you, for your kin, for those with whom you share your hearth. You made a mistake giving her that stone. You need to get it back. You need to avenge your friend. You need to keep your people safe."

I turned away from her and stared at the pyre, lost in thought. I thought about my friend. I thought about something that happened a few years ago, when Sam and I had gone into a mine with the intentions of rescuing a girl from a mad Fae. I thought about Sam carrying me out of that hole in the dirt, a length of bone roughly as long as my pinky jutting out of the meat of my thigh, the girl dead on a stone slab behind us. I thought about the pictures that the Carvers had of my father. I thought about Melly. I thought about my sister and the demon that drove her to suicide. And finally, I thought about the way that every single time, despite having the ability to do things that most people deemed either miraculous or make-believe, I'd failed, and the darkness that killing Cash had birthed started to stir. I'd let myself be a victim for too god damned long.

It was time to make someone else a victim.

"What do I have to do?" I asked.

"Take back the stone."

"Well, that shouldn't be challenging at all. Anything else?"

"Before the Hunter's moon."

"Which is when? No. Wait. Let me guess. Tonight?"

She nodded.

I sighed.

"Awesome."

CHAPTER 30

I left Kari before Canute came back and went straight home.

Once I got inside, I went straight for the room across the hall from my bedroom. The room was empty, the only window covered in a heavy blanket, blocking out the morning sun.

I left my bag in the hall, shut the door behind me, and sat down in the corner. I didn't bother turning the light on. I needed the darkness. I also needed an ally. Someone, or rather, something that I could trust to give me straight answers. To get that, though, I would need to approach said ally on its turf. It made cutting a deal a bit easier.

"Here goes nothing," I muttered, opened the razor and drew it across my hand. I admit it, I'm not a badass. It hurt, but it was necessary. I held the fetish stone in my hand, letting my blood saturate it and let my thoughts drift, clearing my mind and focusing on breathing, on stillness, on just being. I took a lot longer than I had hoped. Every time I tried to clear my head a million different discomforts came creeping in, little aches and pains, nausea, a headache, the fact that I was pouring sweat from just about every square inch of my body, it all pulled my concentration away. Finally, though, I managed to fall into something resembling a rhythm.

Each time I inhaled and exhaled it served as a symbolic renewal, a cleansing of the mind and body. Outside, the sounds of Asheville grew together until each individual noise became a distinct vibration against my ears, each one crystal clear and perfectly pitched in the rhythm of the city. I could feel every dust mote in the air as it settled against my skin, each one exploding with sensation like a tiny electrical charge. I focused on my heartbeat, using it as my own personal drum beat. Each beat, speaking its own note in an internal music, a music that connected me to the world. It was a song of life merging with spirit.

Entering the spirit world leaves your body, essentially, an empty shell. The lights might be on, but there's for sure no one home. As such, if something happens to you in the spirit world and you don't find your way back to your body, then you end up leaving behind an unoccupied meat suit. Assuming someone finds you, chances are they assume you're catatonic. No one finds you, you die. Simple as that. The flip side is also true. Something happens to your spirit—a bigger spirit eats it for instance—Well, you don't have to worry too much about what happens to your body.

I opened my eyes and the room had changed. It was a spiritual equivalent now. A place walled in emotion and thought, lacking any sort of physicality or borders.

I pushed off from the floor, rising through the ceiling with nothing more than a thought, passing into the open air. Beneath me the city was a wash of writhing spirits, large and small, twisting through streets that pulsed with the steady, sleeping breath of the city's own, infinitely larger spirit.

For a long moment, I basked in the feeling of freedom, of weightlessness, of flight. Air elementals, tiny things that vaguely resembled winged snakes made of swirling air drifted past me, caught in invisible updrafts. Below me, the spirit of a church, given form by countless years of faith, prayer, and charity, radiated with an unwavering whitish yellow glow. It was a perfect mirror image of its physical counterpart, yet here it seemed more real, more defined, more alive.

Movement through the spirit world was directed primarily with thought, by focusing on the emotion attached to a place. Doing that, you could reach its spiritual equivalent, for the most part, instantaneously. It wasn't exactly good for spying, and it left you vulnerable, but there were things in the spirit world that were capable of following someone, quite literally, to hell and back. There were spirits here that had been standing on the bank of the big puddle of primordial ooze where we first squirmed out of the muck. That didn't mean it was easy to get their help, or that it came cheap, but sometimes it was worth it.

There were a few spirits I was on good terms with, weaker spirits that didn't have a name, and were more animal than what could be considered a rational, thinking being. For something like this, I needed something with some mojo. Something that, if needed, could actually cross over to the real world.

The only spirits that could do something like that were

the ones that had been around a while. In this case, it was a death spirit that called herself Bec.

More importantly, I knew where she was. She stayed at the hospital, which seems kind of lazy, honestly. Then again, who am I to judge? Instead I focused on the smell of the cleaner in the waiting room's air, the sound of the machines and their constant, monotone beeps, the image of the sick and dying, laid out in a hospital bed. Once I had the mental image firmly in place, it was only a matter of closing my eyes for a brief moment, then opening them to find myself standing outside the emergency room doors.

A hospital in the spirit world is a terrifying place. It's generally a place of healing, or at least that's how we as people tend to think of it. However, we also think of it as a place of sickness and pain. As such, there were spirits crawling all over the exterior of the building, which was, in a way, a spirit in and of itself. Spirits of sickness that looked like Volkswagen-sized bacteria slid over the exterior. Pain spirits, like spiders made entirely out of razor sharp blades crawled back and forth, leaving bleeding cuts along the hospital's walls in their wake. Spirits of healing floated along behind them, pure, white glowing orbs that erased the pain spirit's passing. All in all, it was half disconcerting and half hypnotizing, like most things on this side of the curtain.

The spirits hadn't noticed me yet, which was a good thing. They have a tendency to be rather territorial and unkind to interlopers and uninvited guests. My best bet from here on out was to walk nice and normal, keep my head down, and pray that none of the things crawling around on the building decided to eat my face off.

So, I put my head down, started towards the front door,

and tried to be as inconspicuous as possible. The sound of metal scraping against metal stopped me a second before one of the pain spirits took my head off. Because, of course, something decided to eat my face off.

A spirit of pain, nearly as tall as I was, lowered itself to the ground between the door and me. It looked mostly like a spider, though with a few extra sets of legs. Its body was covered in row upon row of serrated, razor sharp blades. Two glowing embers, set deep inside what I'm assuming was its face, stared at me with a hungry intelligence.

"You're out of your element, Spirit Talker," it said, its voice vaguely reminiscent of the sound of a knife dragged across whetstone.

Around me, more of the pain spirits were settling onto the ground, all of them smaller than the one in front of me, though not by much. They twitched and shifted back and forth, hungry with anticipation.

"I'm not here to cause a problem," I said, trying to keep my voice at a nice even keel.

"No? Then why are you here? Out of your element?"

"Did you just call me Donny?" I asked.

The spirit just stared. Guess they weren't Coen Brothers fans.

"I need to see Bec," I said.

"And I say you don't."

I didn't take my eyes off the spirit, but I became acutely aware that all the others had inched a bit closer to me. Not surprisingly really, given that spirits grow in power by consuming weaker spirits. I was definitely the weaker spirit here. I really needed to change that perspective before I ended up as kibble. Lucky for me, I'd already put that plan into motion.

My life man, I tell ya.

"I've tried being polite. Now stand aside, spirit," I said.

The pain spirits let out a hissing, grating sound. It took me a second to realized they were laughing at me. Assholes.

"And if I choose to disregard your thinly veiled threat, Spirit Talker?"

I took a step forward. The air around me crackled with hungry anticipation.

"Then I'll walk out of here with a new pet," I said.

"Kill it," one of the other spirits said from behind me. Thankfully, the boss ignored it.

"Oh?" the spirit said, lifting one of the six-foot-long blades it called a leg and putting its point to my throat. I stared at the spirit and tried not to move, lest I accidentally force the blade into my spiritual jugular.

"Perhaps I don't want to be your pet," the spirit said. "Perhaps, I am too hungry to be your pet."

I sighed.

"That's too bad really."

Funny thing about Fetishes: once they have a spirit bound to them, they exist on both planes of existence. So, I put my hand into my pocket, the same one I'd cut, and withdrew a hunk of quartz roughly the size of a golf ball. A second later the fire spirit burst out of the fetish, shattering it and launching itself directly into the boss pain spirit's face. That's the other funny thing about Fetishes. In the real world, this would have been about the equivalent of a really loud firecracker. Here though, on their own turf, I was essentially releasing a being of pure flame back into the wild, albeit through another spirit's face.

The fire spirit tore through Mister Crawly Blades, leaving a hole big enough for me to put my fist in, completely through what I still wasn't sure was its head. The other spirits all jumped back, scrambling away. Big bangs and death are scary, even on this side of reality, I suppose. The fire spirit, howling and laughing like mad, sat on the sidewalk, staring up me.

"I did good, right? Right? What you needed? I can go now? No more debt?"

"You did fine. You're free. I release you."

"Good. Good. Make another deal soon? Not bad Spirit Talker. See you soon? Yes?"

"We'll talk," I said.

The spirit nodded eagerly and then took off. He was simply there one minute, and then gone.

I turned to stare up at the hospital. Most of the spirits had paid enough attention to note what had just happened, and then gone back about their business. Either I'd made a point that screwing with me wasn't in their best interest, or they just didn't care. I figured it was probably the latter. Call it a hunch.

"Well," a voice, female and utterly unamused, said from behind me. "I suppose I should find a new doorman now."

"Hi, Bec," I said, turning to face the death spirit.

CHAPTER 31

As far as embodiments of death go, Bec didn't really look that intimidating. She wasn't wearing a cloak, her head wasn't a human skull, and she didn't carry a scythe or have big black wings sticking out of her back. She wasn't dressed like a Viking shield maiden either. She was actually pretty understated, all things considered. I always wondered why that was, why death spirits looked so damn human. Even the Valkyrie that had taken Gus just looked like a woman. A few centuries out of her time, but a woman nonetheless. I guess it made that whole Drag You to the Afterlife thing a little easier to stomach.

Bec looked kind of nerdy, and really, really bored. She was a little over five feet tall, with short blonde hair and glasses. She dressed like a college kid: jeans, black t-shirt, and some old scuffed Chuck Taylors. The only thing that set her apart from looking completely human was her pallor. She had the literal complexion of a corpse, right down to the blue-tinted lips and the milky film of cataracts over her eyes.

"What do you want, Jonah?"

"I came to make a deal, Bec."

"You're serious?"

"Very much so."

"Aren't you up to your neck in deals as it is?"

"Please?"

"No," she said, then considered for a moment before adding, "Hell no."

"Pretty please?"

She stared at me, then turned her head, seemingly taking in everything around us. Finally, she turned back to me and gave an exasperated sigh.

"Fine. But there's a catch," she said.

"Name it."

She quirked a brow.

"You're eager."

"Yeah, it's important."

"The condition is, I have to come for someone soon, someone important to you. When I do, you won't interfere."

That was not entirely a comforting thought. Time in the spirit world worked differently than it did in the physical world. Soon, in her definition, could be anything from five minutes from now to fifty years.

"How soon is soon?" I asked.

"Soon."

"That's not telling me a whole lot."

She shrugged.

"Soon enough that you'll have time with them. Not a lot, but enough."

"Who?" I asked.

She shrugged again.

"That's the catch. You're going to kill someone important to me, and I have to let you?"

"Let me? Awful sure of yourself, aren't you?"

"That's not what I meant."

"I said you don't interfere," she explained, annoyed.

"Do we have a deal?"

I'm not a fan of hard decisions. If I agreed, she'd come and take someone I cared about. That was a pretty short list. I knew she'd be good to her word, too. On the other hand, I may have time to try and figure a way out of it.

"Tell me who."

"No," she said.

"Who?"

"I'm getting annoyed, Jonah."

I knew I couldn't stop Bec when she came for whomever it was that she'd have her sights set on. I didn't know if I'd have time to even make an attempt. I did know that Lysone would do something potentially catastrophic with the Ledberg stone in hand and that time was wasting. The only thing I had control over was how high the body count would be when it was all said and done. Would I be willing to sacrifice someone I cared about to have a chance at stopping her?

I really needed a drink.

"Deal," I said, quietly.

She nodded once.

"What do you need?"

"Information, essentially."

"What exactly does essentially mean?"

"There's a woman. She has a stone. I need to find her."

"Why?"

"I owe her," I said.

"And I'm pretty sure you're wrong."

"How so?"

Bec shook her head.

"You've set things in motion that are outside of my control, even if I wanted to intervene."

Bec stared at me, lips pressed tight together in a thin line.

"Is there something I'm not seeing here?"

"Seriously, Jonah? You? Miss something right in front of your face? You're right. I must be talking crazy, you'd never do that."

"So what is it then?"

Bec shook her head again.

"I can't. It's bigger than me."

"You can't tell me."

"Not my place. Bigger players on the board and I'm not stepping on toes," she said, which did nothing to help my comfort level. "Now, what else, Jonah?"

"I need you to watch someone for me. Make sure they are safe until I can get to them. I have a plan, but I need time."

"Who?"

"My old man."

She nodded.

"There's some bad folk that may be paying him a visit. Can you do that? Keep him whole for me?"

Bec nodded.

"Is that it?" she asked.

"That's it."

"Wow," she said, a look of smug self-satisfaction on her face.

I gave her a cold stare.

"Run along, Jonah," she said, making a shooing motion with her hand. "It seems I've got stuff to do."

"Thanks Bec," I said, finally.

"Go, damn," she said, though she still sounded more bored than irritated.

I figured I'd taken enough chances for one day, and turned my thoughts towards my home.

I came back to the physical world with a sharp gasp of air. My back ached from being propped against the wall. I opened my hand, and the stone was now dust mixed with blood, creating a sticky black mess in my palm. My shirt was all but plastered to my body with sweat, my leg ached, and I was getting one bitch of a migraine. All in all, though, I was pretty sure nothing was broken. I could've used a drink, granted, but I'd come back whole. Given the way things had been going for me, I took that as a win.

I checked my watch. I'd been in the spirit world for a whopping total of five minutes. It was damn disorienting. It felt like I'd been there for hours.

I had a little while, I figured, before Bec got back to me. If anyone would be able to find Lysone, it would be her. Like I said, death spirits aren't exactly lightweights. In the meantime, I needed a few hours of sleep, and then to handle a few things. I didn't want to admit to myself that a few of them were in case I didn't come back. Strange thing was, now that I'd made up my mind, I wasn't really afraid. Whatever happened from here on out, happened.

Somewhere along the line, I made my peace with that. In the end, all that mattered was that Lysone paid for what she did to Gus.

I took a few minutes to load my bag with all sorts of fun herbs, fetishes, and one or two other parlor tricks and hit the road.

CHAPTER 32

I pulled into the parking lot at the Poor Confederate, killed the engine, and stared at the exterior of the bar for a long, long time. There were other cars in the small gravel lot, most of them beaten-down relics from a few decades back. None of them would qualify as classics, and that was being generous. A few of them were literally held together with duct tape and zip ties. I was a little surprised. It wasn't even dark yet.

I didn't bother thinking it over. Hell, a few days ago I had been nothing but exposed nerves and anxiety heading in here. Now, honestly, I wouldn't say this was the least of my worries, but it sure wasn't at the top of the list.

I grabbed the bags of gold jewelry and watches that Gus had left me and the cash from Lysone, shoved it in the front pocket of my sweatshirt, grabbed a few small things out of my bag, and climbed out of my truck.

Apparently, the rednecks had been carpooling. The interior was standing room only, a sea of denim and flannel as far as the eye could see. One of the Hank Williamses was playing over the jukebox, droning on about drugs and women. The entire place smelled of cigarette smoke (the legal and illegal kind), sweat, and beer, to the point that it felt like the air itself had grown thick and sticky.

Waylon was sitting in his back booth with a few other guys, all of them clad in jeans and cowboy boots. The two opposite of Waylon wore country western shirts, the kind with the pearl buttons and flowers embroidered into them. Waylon wore a black t-shirt, sans sleeves. He said something that set the other two to laughing, then took a sip of his beer and lit a cigarette. After another moment or two of conversation, his two compatriots stood up and left, shaking hands with him before they departed.

They passed within a few inches of me on their way out the door. For a second the air felt cooler, but I didn't bother to pay it any real attention. I had bigger things to do.

I walked to Waylon's table and dropped into the seat across from him. A very quick look of surprise crossed his face, but he masked it just as quickly, taking another long pull from his cigarette. He settled back into the booth, took a sip of his beer, and stared at me.

"Jonah," he said finally. "Was wondering when I'd see you again."

I didn't respond. He narrowed his eyes, appraising me in the dim lighting.

"There's something different about you, Jonah."

I took the pouch of gold out of my sweatshirt, along with the cash, and dropped them in the center of the table.

Waylon raised an eyebrow.

"And this is?"

"Your money," I said, surprising myself at how steady my voice sounded.

Waylon picked up the cash and flipped through it, then shoved the whole stack into his pocket. Next, he picked up the bag and peeked inside. He gave it a little shake, the contents rattling, then sighed and put it back on the table. He sat there for a minute, tapping one finger on the tabletop and smoking his cigarette.

"You know, Jonah, I gotta give you credit for your initiative, son."

"I'm not your son," I said.

Waylon quirked a brow. The way he looked at me changed. There was a bit of wariness.

"And thank God for that."

I didn't respond.

"Problem is," Waylon continued, "I run a cash-only business."

"That sounds like your problem," I said. "I'm paid up."

Waylon looked like he'd been slapped in the face.

"Pardon?"

"I said that's your problem."

"Well, I can't say I find this change of attitude very becoming of you. I might find it in me to be insulted."

"I'm too tired for your crap right now, Waylon," I said, and I sounded it.

"That right?"

I nodded towards the pouch on the table.

"Take it. We're square."

"Well, tired or not, like I said, I run a cash business. Now, I can count that towards say, I don't know, twenty percent of the balance, but—"

"Stop talking."

If Waylon looked like he'd been slapped earlier, now he looked like I'd slapped his mother.

"We're paid up. That's more than what I owe you. You know people that can turn that into cash. I'm not doing this crap with you anymore, Waylon. We're done."

Waylon snuffed his cigarette out on the table and dropped the butt on the floor. He slid his mostly empty beer glass to the side and leaned forward, staring into my face.

"Listen to me, you little son of a bitch—"

"No," I said, interrupting him. "You listen. You and your brother have threatened me, hounded me, sent me to the hospital, threatened to off my father, and generally just been complete and utter douchebags."

Waylon opened his mouth to say something.

"I'm not finished."

Surprisingly enough, Waylon shut his mouth.

"It works like this. We're squared up now. If you come near me again," I said, leaning forward so we were almost face to face. I kept my hands in the front pocket of my sweatshirt. "I will play hell on your life in ways you don't even think are possible."

"Was that a threat?" Waylon asked through clenched teeth. I was pretty sure, in his entire life, no one had ever spoken to Waylon Carver like that. The pure rage radiating off him was palpable. His face had gone an almost unnatural shade of red. A vein stood out on his forehead, and both of his hands had clenched into tight fists on the tabletop.

"Yeah, actually now that I think about it, it was," I said.

"You done screwed up," Waylon said.

"Yeah?" I asked, pulling my hands out of my pocket.

"Yeah," Waylon said, standing.

I didn't answer. Instead, I slapped him in the face. Hard. In the bar, even over the music, it sounded like a pistol shot. Heads turned towards us, half of them slack jawed and surprised that someone had just walked in here and slapped the boss. Blood streaked his face. Not his, mine. I'd been working up a little something for just this occasion.

Shamans have used hallucinogenic herbs for ceremonies, dream walking, vision quests and a million other reasons for as long as there's been magic to play with. Given law enforcement's view on said substances, the most powerful were really, really hard to come by. The ayahuasca had cost me several hundred dollars for a few milligrams, and by itself it wasn't that potent. South American tribes would mix it with other herbs and use it for healing and divination. With my blood and my intent behind it, activating its inherent magic, just the vine itself would make the Brown Acid from Woodstock look like a happy daydream. Within seconds the magic would take hold and it would cause Waylon to see any multitude of different planes of existence, up to and including the spirit world, heaven, and hell.

It took less than a second. Waylon's eyes widened, pupils filling out and overtaking the normal gray color of his eyes. He opened his mouth to scream, but it was silent, his face pulled into a rictus grin of pure terror. He fell back into the booth, his body taut, trembling.

I grabbed the pouch of gold off the table, leaned over and put it in his hand and stood.

"Told you so," I said, grabbing a napkin off the table and clenching it tightly in my fist.

I grabbed my cane and headed towards the door, item number one on my to-do list thoroughly and decisively marked off.

CHAPTER 33

I was unlocking the door to my truck when Bec appeared, sitting in the passenger seat. She looked mostly translucent. I could see the shopping center near the Poor Confederate through her. Given that she was materializing in the real world, she wouldn't be able to hang around for long. Even for a spirit as powerful as her, maintaining this was taxing as hell. I slid into the truck beside her, and started the engine.

"I found who you're looking for," she told me, her voice sounding far away, like she was talking to me from the bottom of a well.

"Where?"

Images flashed through my mind. Trees. A paved hiking path. A cave. A stone profile similar to a face, against a sunset-painted sky. I knew the place.

The Devil's Courthouse.

It was very, very cliché.

The Devil's Courthouse had its fair share of urban legends surrounding it. The devil held court in the caves within the mountain, being amongst the most colorful. The Cherokee believed that there was a giant that lived there. A few scholars had disagreed, but the legends had stuck. The local fare, strange noises at night, people seeing apparitions and all manner of oddball things kept the stories alive.

The images faded as quickly as they had come.

"My old man? The girl with him?"

"Both safe and sound," Bec said.

I turned towards the passenger seat, to thank her again. Of course, it was empty. I took a deep breath, shook my head to clear it, and put the truck in gear. Something was going on inside the Poor Confederate, judging from the number of people that had started filing out of the door, most of them moving at a full-on run. The screaming and the wailing sirens in the distance sort of tipped me off, too.

I didn't hang around. I figured the screaming, running, and sirens had something to do with Waylon and, as such, I should make myself scarce.

I spent what little time I had driving towards the Devil's Courthouse. I wasn't entirely sure where Lysone was going to be, but I had a hunch. Most spells that require a certain natural event, an eclipse, a storm, or what have you, had to be done in view of said event. Kari had mentioned the moon so I figured in full view was about as good as it got.

That would mean a long half-mile hike to the top. On foot. My leg was already aching at the thought. Most folks without a bum leg and a cane would consider the hike strenuous. For me, with a bad pin, it was going to be quite the climb.

It took me the better part of an hour to reach the observation deck, but it was well worth it. The view was pretty stellar. Supposedly, from where I was standing, beside a waist-high stone wall, you could see into Tennessee, South Carolina, and Georgia. The rock face jutted out in front of me. There were a few folks, couples mostly, wandering around and taking in the view, but from what I could see there was no sign of Lysone.

It dawned on me while I was standing there that, while I'd been all set to do this, I had nothing that even remotely resembled a plan. I had time, though. I'd gotten here first, which gave me a chance to set things up before Lysone got here to enact whatever this spell was.

I was going to have to hit her hard, fast, and I'd probably only get a chance to do it once. I started to take stock of my surroundings, and of my situation. I was in a location that was mostly natural, thus if I needed a spiritual ally of some sort, my choices were mostly elementals or animal. Neither were easy to deal with, though the animal spirits were worse. They were, outside of the oldest and most powerful, direct as all hell. They served their nature. It pretty much came down to eat, sleep, reproduce, rinse and repeat.

I walked away from the observation deck and into the trees, letting my mind wander. I was mostly just waiting for an idea to hit me, taking in the scenery as I went. Fading sunlight filtered in through the trees, casting a warm, golden glow over everything. I used my cane, turning over rocks and brushing aside sticks as I went.

I was maybe three hundred yards into the tree line when I found exactly what I was looking for. The yellow jacket nest was nestled under a rocky outcropping and it was, for lack of a better term, freaking huge. Nearly a foot high, twice as long, and all but covered with the violent little yellow-and-black, six-legged assholes of nature.

I found a small log and sat down, resting my leg and watching the wasps mill about the nest. Mainly, I wanted to rest for a minute, but it wouldn't hurt me to get my head straight before I broke on through to the other side and started making even more deals with spirits.

After a few moments, I settled my head back, closed my eyes, and let my consciousness drift. Given that time passed differently on the other side, I had to be quick about this. Five minutes could pass here and it would feel like hours in the spirit world. On the flip side, hours could pass on this side and it feel like five minutes on the other side. The last thing I wanted to do was go through all this trouble, only to pop back over here after the party had already ended.

When I opened my eyes, I was fully in the spirit world. It was more primordial here, due to the fact that I was in surroundings that were definitively more natural. Trees towered overhead, each one adorned with leaves as big as dinner plates or pine needles the length of drum sticks, reaching into a sky the color of sapphires. In the distance, I heard bird song so beautiful and clear that it was almost painful to hear. A butterfly, its wings each a perfect kaleidoscope of greens and purples, drifted by lazily.

The hive sat directly across from me. Its spirit world equivalent was massive, at least double what it was in the physical world. The outside had been crafted with intricate whorls and twists, giving it an artistic bent that was strangely ordered and hypnotic if you stared at it too long.

I took a few steps towards the hive, making sure my

movements were slow and without any sort of intent that could be construed as threatening. It got their attention. An angry buzzing sound, the sound of thousands upon thousands of insect wings coming alive in unison filled the air. They started pouring out of the nest, each one as long as my finger, creating a massive black cloud of spiritual, winged nastiness for nastiness' sake in the air in front of me.

The yellow jackets formed a sphere around me, the sound of their combined wings near deafening. When they spoke, it was as a single entity, each hornet's voice a small part of a much larger, and much louder whole.

"You have disturbed the hive. Why?" the thousands of voices asked.

"I seek an audience with your queen," I said.

"For what purpose?" The voices came again.

"I need help," I said.

"Seek it elsewhere," they said.

"Then an arrangement," I said.

"To what purpose?"

"I told you, I wish to speak to your queen. Not you."

The swarm buzzed angrily, twisting and writhing over itself, yet still holding the spherical shape around me. I could smell something in the air, pheromones, or the spiritual equivalent. It smelled odd, like wood smoke and burning sugar.

The buzzing increased, and through the swarm, I saw a shape roughly the size of a large house cat rise up out of the hive. The swarm separated and the queen of the hive flew into the sphere of hornets, the massive wall of thought-formed insects closing behind her. She stopped, hovering just a few inches from my face.

The queen of the hive was beautiful. Sure, she looked like a giant winged distributor of pain and misery, but her colors, the yellow and black stripes, were brighter, more alive than the real-world counterpart. Her wings threw out flashes of color, reflecting the sunlight back like prisms. It was her eyes though, that really got me. They were black, almost mirror-like, but they held an almost frightening level of intelligence. The queen's stinger was exposed, a six-inch spike of obsidian black. Venom dripped from its tip, each drop smoking as it hit the ground, eating away at the soil, only for the earth spirits in the ground to fill in the hole almost instantaneously.

"You have our attention," the queen said.

CHAPTER 34

I offered the queen of the yellow jackets a bow.

"Your majesty," I said. "I need your help."

"To what ends? We are only listening because of your stupidity, not your social graces."

"I'll take what I can get," I said.

"Speak your piece, Spirit Talker," the queen said.

"There's a woman coming here. She has something I mean to take. I need your help to do such."

"And that is our concern how?"

"Because I'm coming to you for an arrangement, not a handout."

The queen's head tilted to the side. Okay, maybe not tilted. It's probably easier to say it rotated a full forty-five degrees.

"What arrangement?" the queen asked.

"A mutually beneficial one," I said. "A tribute to your hive. Food, perhaps? For the winter?"

There was a murmur of wings and the queen drifted

closer to me. One of her antennae twitched ever so slightly. Her head rotated in the opposite direction, mandibles clacking against each other with a hungry intensity.

"Perhaps we will take you as tribute, payment for disturbing us?"

"Perhaps," I said with a slight shrug. This was exactly how I'd expected this conversation to go. Hornets, by their nature, are territorial creatures. On this side of the metaphysical fence, that was just amped up to eleven. I'd walked onto their turf and asked for a meeting with the boss, no introductions, no nothing.

"Unfortunately, you don't understand how my world works," I said.

The queen's head rotated in the opposite direction. The smell of pheromones got thicker. If I were standing in the physical world, I'd probably be gagging.

"Perhaps you should not assume that we care?" the queen said.

"Maybe you don't. You could have your hive kill my other body," I said, nodding back towards my actual physical body, which was propped against a tree. To most anyone that passed, I'd just look like I was asleep. Granted, I was pretty sure no one would venture this far off the path. If they did, they'd hear the nest long before they saw it. The buzzing chorus of a couple thousand of nature's flying douchebags would be more than enough to keep any intelligent person back. I tried not to think about what that said about my levels of stability.

"But you should," I said, matter of fact.

The queen stared at me.

"You sting me over there, somebody will find me.

They'll need to remove my carcass. That means they'll have to torch your nest. You off me here, I'll sit there until I starve, or someone finds me. End result is the same. To get me out, your nest has gotta go. We both know what that means. There's a balance, one side affects the other."

Which was the plain and simple truth. The spirit world was, essentially, a reflection of sorts of the physical world. There was a symbiotic relationship between the two planes of existence. Something here dies, it affects my side of things. For instance, if the queen were to die, the hive in the real world might die. If they were to destroy the nest in the real world, it would have consequences here. The buzzing got louder, becoming almost deafening. I could feel the motion of several thousands of wings, like a light breeze washing over my body. Some sort of communication passed through the hive, unheard by me. Finally, the queen drifted forward, the venom from her stinger falling less than a foot away from my toes, each drop leaving a bubbling, smoking hole in the earth. I curled my toes up in my shoes, just in case.

"Make your offer," the queen said finally.

"Tribute, as I told you."

"In what form?"

"You help me. Harm my enemy on my behalf and your children, in my world, will eat for the winter."

"And how will such an arrangement benefit me? I will likely die before the first of the cold. I am old."

At this point, I was willing to agree to whatever she wanted. I only needed the yellow jackets to act as a distraction. I had no doubt that Lysone would make short work of the queen's physical equivalent and her hive. So, I really didn't have to honor any deal that I made.

"Your hive continues," I said. "You and your brood get to keep humming along and irritating the shit out of tourists."

"There is more I want," the queen said. "A tribute of your essence."

I quirked a brow.

A shaman's blood is where their magic lies. It's how I'm able to do the work I do. It, in its own right, is pretty potent stuff, especially to a spirit. It was the equivalent of a permanent steroidal boost to whatever spirit consumed it. If I gave up a bit of the red stuff, the queen would grow exponentially in power. Not a bad thing if she was my ally. It also meant I'd have to climb that damn hill up here every so often in the winter, in the cold, the snow and the ice, on a pretty regular basis until spring. A small price to pay to not get turned into a bloodstain when it was all said and done.

"Consider it done," I said.

"Very well," the queen said. "We will aid you. Now go."

I didn't hang around to argue. I took a moment to focus, and when I opened my eyes I was back in the real world. The sun hung low in the sky, just above the horizon.

That didn't leave me a lot of time. I cut the palm of my hand, and held it out, open and outstretched. Within a matter of seconds, it was crawling with yellow jackets which, while being damn disconcerting, was kind of a rush. A moment later, they flew back to their nest, my palm cleaned of blood.

CHAPTER 35

I didn't have a lot more prep time before Lysone showed up to concoct whatever concoction she was planning on concocting. Though, truth be told, there wasn't much preparation to be done. I grabbed up a few herbs, shoved them into my bag and found a place a bit off the trail, but with a sight line that enabled me to watch the comings and goings along the path. For the most part, all I got to see were a few hikers, a few families with their kids, and the random hippie.

It wasn't until the sun had finally settled behind the horizon that I saw Lysone.

I was surprised at first glance. I expected her to appear in a flash of lightning, or maybe step out of a pillar of flame, at the very least come strolling out of some fog. I hadn't expected to see her, with the aura of power that surrounded her, trudging up the path with a backpack thrown over one shoulder, sweating and panting like the rest of us average Joes.

Come to think of it, I'd expected to feel that wash of power long before I saw her. Instead, I didn't feel a damn thing. Not so much as an inkling of the power I'd felt before.

Curious.

I watched her as she trudged up the hill, hopped the wall, and wandered out on the large, rocky outcropping. She took the bag off her shoulder and put it at her feet, sat down and took a bottle of water out of her bag. She took a few sips of the water and started pulling things out of her pack, laying them on the stone around her.

Ritual magic, like what I was assuming she was about to do, took time and concentration. I figured my best course of action was to wait until she got into mid-mojo, unleash the swarm, and then hit her with everything I had in one hard, quick sucker punch. Hopefully, that'd be enough to put an end to all this nonsense.

Lysone started the ritual as a massive moon the color of dried blood started to lift into the sky. She'd spent the better part of a half an hour prepping for it. From what I'd been able to see from where I sat, the stone sat at the center of it. There was a cross of some sort, or a compass, drawn on the rocks in red. She set bowls at each of the eight points, each of them containing what I assumed was some type of herb. From what I could piece together, or at least based on what I knew of magical theory, she'd light each in turn, using them to collect energy and direct it towards the center, towards the stone.

She'd have to keep her focus throughout the course of the ritual, to be able to channel and control that much energy, regardless of how much power she had. If I hit her right around the time she lit the sixth or seventh bowl, that should go pretty far in ensuring that whatever chain reaction I set off was pretty spectacular. I'd probably want to ensure I wasn't standing too close when such a thing went down, but one problem at a time.

I watched her, hidden in the boughs of an oak tree a bit off the path, and opened up my senses, letting the spirit world come flooding in. Almost instantly, I was bombarded with the various strings of power she was pulling together, each one a bright green so unnatural in shade that it reminded me of toxic waste. I'd seen the way my magic worked and this was different, twisted. What I did was tap into the power of life, of growth. Lysone's was a perversion of that, like she'd at one point had what I had, only it had been corrupted in a way that I couldn't understand. That pretty much put to rest the idea that whatever it was she was working was good, compassionate, and kindly. This was the sort of color that went with sickness, madness, and disease.

What surprised me, however, was her aura. The size of an aura was strictly based on how much of a connection a person had with the spirit world. Mine, for instance, probably radiated out from my body a few inches. Same thing for most humans with an innate connection to the spirit world or those capable of working magic. A werewolf, for instance, who was very closely tied to the spirit world, having two spirits and all, had auras radiated out a few feet. The Fae, their auras were damned near blinding.

The way the aura moved and its colors were tied to a person's mood, personality, and so on and so forth. Bottom line, you could tell a lot about a person from reading their aura.

Lysone's was near non-existent, barely more than an outline, which went completely counter to the power I had felt radiating off her earlier. There was no two ways around it. She was completely, utterly, and benignly human, which made absolutely not a bit of sense. On the plus side, the way her aura moved around her frame, twisting and whirling on itself, was a telltale sign of insanity, so at least I'd been right on that account.

Lysone pulled the ropes of power together, twisting them into a single sphere of energy. As she did, she chanted in a language I didn't know. From the few words and phrases I caught, it sounded Germanic. It had a music all its own, a lilting melody that helped her focus and pull the strands of energy in towards her. For someone with no real magical power of their own, she was doing a pretty good job of making it work.

I waited until she lit the sixth bowl to step out from my hidey-hole. The concentration it took to maintain the spell was written on her face. I could've rode in on an elephant with a marching band accompaniment without her noticing I was there.

I'd spent more than a few minutes thinking over how I'd break her concentration enough for the spell to go haywire and cause her as much physical pain as possible. Up until now, I didn't think I could hurt her. The fact that she was every bit as much flesh and bone as I was, and just as vulnerable, caused a smile to spread out across my face that was so wide it almost hurt. At the same time, somewhere deep down, far away and distant, a touch of conscience drifted up, reminding me of how I'd felt after I'd killed Cash, how that was still hanging around me. I ignored it.

I was going to give to her far worse than she gave to my friend. I was going to take that damned rock. I wasn't sure what I was going to do with it once I got it, but that was the plan nonetheless.

I reached into my bag and pulled out the dandelion I'd picked. Dandelion, as it goes, only has a few real uses, and those are mostly associated with the root. Though, for what I had in mind, the roots weren't going to do much for me. I needed the leaves. The leaves could be used for a few different things: summonings, divination, and the like. I needed them for their tie to the winds.

I cut my hand with my pocketknife as I walked, letting the blood soak into the leaves and gathering up my intent. I waited until I'd hopped the wall, and tossed the leaves towards Lysone. In the spirit world, it looked like I'd tossed a handful of burning embers into the air. They drifted upwards and vanished a few feet away from me.

A wind spirit, drawn by the magic I'd released and my intent, came swooping out of the sky, wings outstretched. It looked, at least to me, like a much smaller version of Quetzalcoatl, the feathered serpent god of South American mythology. Granted, small was relative. This thing was at least ten feet long with a wingspan that was easily twice that.

In the physical world, a gust of wind that was nearing hurricane force tore through the trees. Leaves, dirt, rocks, and just about anything that wasn't nailed down were lifted into the air and thrown around with violent ferocity. This included the bowls that Lysone was using for her ritual. I couldn't help but wonder what would happen if one of those little burning embers fell on a pile of dried leaves, then disregarded the thought every bit as quickly as it had come. Either way, imminent forest fire or not, the wind sufficed to break Lysone's concentration and a shockwave of energy rippled out from the center of the circle, hitting me full on in the chest. It wasn't anywhere near as bad as I figured it would be, more like getting hit in the center of the chest with a massive pillow. Though, when I looked down, I noticed that all the plants, moss, and trees within twenty yards had completely withered. Magic's funny like that.

The wind faded as quickly as it had come, leaving Lysone sitting on her knees in the middle of the outcropping. She didn't so much as bother to turn around. She just sat there, hands palm down over her knees, head slightly lowered.

"Do you have any idea what you've done?" she asked, her voice quiet.

"Honestly, I haven't the foggiest. I figure, though, that it's in my best interest to screw it all up."

Lysone stood up and turned towards me. In that instant, that wash of familiar, terrifying power came crashing into me. Her aura, which, until seconds ago, was nearly nonexistent suddenly grew exponentially and something in my head, something I hadn't even realized until just now, clicked into place.

Her power wasn't hers. It was borrowed. Someone or something else was giving her mojo on loan. Not that it mattered, really. A borrowed gun can kill you just as dead.

"You don't understand," she said, stalking towards me.

"We've established that," I said.

"This is necessary," she growled.

I took a few steps backwards, the back of my knees hitting the small stone wall that separated the rocky outcropping from the rest of the trail.

"If you're referring to causing me bodily harm, it's really not," I said.

"Oh, I will cause you harm," she said, and her voice kicked down a notch, taking on an almost sultry purr. "I will cause you so much harm."

CHAPTER 36

Lysone came at me, pure rage and malice in motion. This wasn't the type of attack you'd associate with someone who, only a minute before, was working some serious magic despite having a complete lack of talent. This was unbridled fury given form.

I tried to move, but I didn't really have the coordination to get out of the way without tripping over my own two feet. All I really did was make a better target out of myself.

Lysone hit me with a tackle that was on par with what I'd expect out of a pro-level linebacker, sending me tumbling over the small rock wall and to the concrete walking path behind it. I hit hard, scraping a good several inches of skin off my elbows and my back. She stepped over the wall after me, hair hanging in her face, and grabbed me by the throat, lifting me up without even the slightest bit of effort. Her hand was vise-like, shutting off the oxygen and blood to my brain. I started thrashing, my hands beating against her arm. If it hurt her in the slightest, she didn't show it.

"Did you really think you could take the key from me?" she growled.

I replied with something that came out like "gurk."

Lysone slapped me with her free hand, and I felt a tooth shake loose.

"That I would just let you take it from me, after all this time?"

She slapped me again, on the opposite side of my face. My eye started swelling shut, a small cut over my eyebrow pouring blood down the side of my cheek. The stitched-together parts of my face had come undone, the thread snapping under the pure blunt force of each hit.

"You poor, misguided, stupid little man," she said, tossing me to the ground with a disappointed shake of her head. Tossed in this case meant being thrown for about thirty feet of skipping and bouncing across the walking trail that led up to the viewing area, just in case I had any skin left that she felt the need to relieve me of.

I didn't get up. The horizon was currently switching between horizontal and vertical at a dizzying pace. I could see her, with my still-open eye, stomping towards me, pure rage and bad intention drawn on the features of her face.

For the second time in as many days, I was fighting for my life. Maybe the incident with Cash made it easier, but there wasn't a whole lot of apprehension left in me when it came to causing someone bodily harm.

Once I came to a stop, I jammed a hand into my bag, sucking in big gulping mouthfuls of air, and grabbed the first thing I could get my hands on. I wasn't entirely sure what it was, and honestly, I didn't care. I spit a mouthful of blood (and a molar) into my palm, focused a whole lot of bad intent towards whatever it was I was holding, and threw it directly into Lysone's face when she got close. It took a moment, but when I realized what I'd hit her with, a small surge of hope ran over my nerves. I might have a dog in this fight after all.

Oleander is a nasty, nasty plant. Sure, it's pretty. Hell, the flowers even smell kind of nice. Like most things in nature, however, it has its unpleasantries, for lack of a better word. In this case, it was that every single part of the plant, from the roots to the pretty pink flowers, to the leaves and stems, were poisonous as all hell. Poisonous enough that there are urban legends about campers and boy scouts skewering their hot dogs with oleander sticks and keeling over dead. The symptoms included nausea, vomiting, severe stomach pain, seizures, comas, and well, death. Personally, I'd have been happy with just about any combination of those.

Fortunately for me, my blood mixed with the herb amped up its magical properties, along with its toxicity. Oleander was one of those plants that, magically, can be used for good or ill, depending on the intent of the person using it. Since my intention was leaning towards the latter, there was a whole lot of hurt to be had.

Lysone doubled over almost instantly, clutched her stomach and broke into one of the most mind-shattering displays of projectile vomiting it has ever been my displeasure to witness. Which, given my history with the sauce, was saying something.

I got to my feet, still dizzy, and shuffled towards the outcropping and the runestone.

Whatever power that Lysone had gotten her hands into

was fighting off the effects of the oleander. She stood up, shook her head, and wiped her mouth on the back of her hand. It seemed like a minor inconvenience that, in the end, had only pissed her off.

I was maybe ten feet from Lysone when she managed to get it together enough to lock her eyes on me. She held up one hand, flicked her wrist, and my feet left the ground. This time, when I landed, it was with an explosion of pain that can't be put into words. My breath caught in my chest, pure liquid fire filling my lungs. I could taste more blood in the back of my throat. I bounced once, and Lysone directed my flight with her hand, slamming me into the ground and then sending me skidding over the ground again, over gravel and roots, until my shoulder came into direct contact with the trunk of a pine tree. There was a loud cracking, which I assumed was my collarbone shattering, and pain lanced through my neck and shoulder, running all the way down to my fingertips. Another motion of her hand and I was pulled back towards her, right across the ground.

Lysone held me there, hovering an inch off the ground with nothing but a stare, and then tossed me out onto the outcropping. She knelt down, picked up my bag, calmly walked towards me and tossed it at my feet. I was only three or four feet at most from the stone, with an entire magical arsenal at my feet. All I could do was lay there, coughing up blood, with a shoulder that, now that I'd bothered to look at it, was crushed into a shape that wasn't even remotely natural.

"Go on," she said. "Take the stone, take up arms, stop me."

I fought up to my hands and knees, trying to hold the

arm with the busted shoulder as close to me as possible. Given that I couldn't really move said arm that in and of itself was a challenge.

"That's it. Go on," she said, her voice full of malicious amusement and dripping with arrogance. "Crawl."

I started to crawl forward and managed to make it about six inches before she brought her foot down across the back of my leg, snapping both bones above my ankle with her heel.

I screamed. My eyes filled with tears, a supernova of pain exploding up my leg. I rolled over onto my side, doubling up into a fetal position.

"Aw, did that hurt?" she asked, giggling.

I reached for my ankle, a simple reflexive action meant to shield my newest wound. She brought her heel down again, this time on my hand, crushing it between her heel and the rock beneath it.

This time, it didn't even hurt. There was just a distant, throbbing cold sensation.

Lysone knelt down beside me, putting her lips right next to my ear.

"I told you. I told you you'd fail," she whispered. "And you'll die. It's inevitable, but not immediate. First the girl, then your friend, the fighter, then your father. I'll make you watch every one of them go before you."

I wanted to tell her she could do something that involved self-copulation and a chainsaw. Instead, I just grinned, a wide, toothy, bloody grin.

Lysone was so caught up in her taunts that she didn't hear what I heard.

It was magical, that sound, the buzzing drone of thousands of sets of insectoid wings in flight.

The swarm of yellow jackets poured out of the tree line, a cloud of pure, all natural, six-legged winged, living embodiments of malice with nothing on their little insect minds but causing some poor, miserable bastard a whole lot of hurt. The yellow jackets poured towards Lysone, engulfing her in a black cloud. Within seconds, her screams mixed with the near constant hum of the yellow jackets' wings. Hornets continued to blow past me for a good few seconds, replacing those that had died after stinging her. Already, a small pile of them had begun to form around her feet.

Lysone thrashed, fighting against the swarm. She stumbled backwards, her screams choked off, and fell against the stone. She twitched a few times and finally went still.

As much as I wanted to just lay my head against the stone, close my eyes, and sleep, die, slip into coma, something, I still needed to get the stone. The best I could do was use my one good leg and my elbow to crawl towards it.

"Shaman!" Kari shouted from behind me.

I rolled over just time to see Lysone slowly getting to her feet. A horde of yellow jackets, all dead, sloughed off of her and pattered against the ground. She was covered from head to toe in swollen, red welts, a few of them bleeding, giving her entire form a twisted, misshapen appearance. Already the wounds were vanishing, though she looked more than a little unsteady on her feet, which, while being nowhere near enough, was at least a small victory on my part.

Kari was several yards behind her, running towards

us, a vague outline against the trees. The massive shape of Canute loped along beside her. She was yelling something after my name, but I couldn't make it out.

I made a maddened dive for the stone, pushing off with my one semi-good leg at the same time that Lysone launched herself towards me. I fell on top of the stone, rolling to the side out of instinct, a split second before Lysone's stompy foot would have found the back of my skull. Instead, she grabbed my hair, and rammed the back of my head into the stone. With that one impact, the pain went away, became so distant that it was nothing more than a memory. I saw another shape behind her, one that I could make out.

I knew who it was.

Bec.

Lysone lifted my head again and I could hear the blood, my blood, spatter against the stone.

She'd killed me. My body just hadn't caught up to that fact just yet.

And then I had a thought.

I had no idea if it would work, but I figured I was dead already, so what the hell. I touched my broken hand to her face, to one of the bleeding stings, and put forth a final, last ditch effort of focused intent.

Shamans have long been regarded as healers, able to cure maladies, both physical and spiritual. Anyone in the know knew that we could take another person's pain, injuries, and ailments into ourselves. It's how Gretchen had been able to heal my father. For obvious reasons, it wasn't something I did often. I was too self-centered to suffer for someone else. What most people in the know weren't aware of was where we could place that pain. With effort, we could take those same injuries, those same maladies and transfer them to someone else. Every single punch I'd taken. Every single kick, cut, bruise, fracture, and tiny tidbit of nuclear pain I'd received over the last few days, I gave every last one of them to Lysone.

Almost immediately I was greeted with a feeling that I can only compare to an opiate high. It was like floating, like warmth, pain simply sliding off my body. I could hear the sound of bones snapping, both back together and apart. Somewhere, Lysone was screaming. I could hear Kari screaming, too. The sound of blood stopped.

Lysone's face, where my own was cut, split open. She dropped me, and I could see her hand, the fingers snapping back at odd angles even as I felt my own knit and snap back into place.

After that, images came in flashes. There was Lysone falling next to me, her eyes open, lips slightly parted, a small line of blood sliding down over her cheek. I felt a building of power, heat against my chest where I was holding the tablet, and then something cold. A frigid, arctic cold spreading out over my chest. I saw the sky, a lance of lightning the same color as the energy Lysone had been manipulating, shoot towards the sky.

I heard words, far away and distant. Kari's voice.

"You did it. You've set him free."

After that, everything went dark.

CHAPTER 37

When I came to, I was in the hospital. Again.

I was alone, the lights were dim, and outside a pale full moon was casting bars of bluish white light over the bed. I laid there like that for a long time, staring up at the ceiling tiles. The only bit of pain I experienced was the dull throbbing in my leg, a gentle thudding ache that, since it had been with me for years, was almost comforting.

I wasn't sure what time it was when the nurse walked in, but the sun was starting to break over the mountains.

"Nice to see you're awake," she said, her accent decidedly Northern.

"Uh, what day is it?"

She pointed towards a little white board stuck on the wall. I read it.

"Thursday?"

"Mhm."

I read the board again.

"So that would make you Amy?"

"In the flesh. How are you feeling?"

"Tired. Very, very tired."

"Makes sense, you were dehydrated, exhausted. When was the last time you slept?"

"Day or two," I said.

"Must've been a tough couple of days," she said, checking a few more things around the room.

"You have no idea."

"Alright Mr. Heywood. Your wife and in-laws are in the hall. I'll send them in."

She was out the door before I had a chance to voice my rather sudden surprise, or extraneous objections, for that matter.

A moment later, Mama Duvalier walked in with a girl, who, until she walked in the room, I thought had been a corpse. For a dead woman, Maryse looked like she was in pretty good shape. I sat up on the bed, trying to make as much distance between myself and Mama Duvalier as I could. Adrenaline hit my system and the heart rate monitor started bleating out a staccato repetition.

Mama Duvalier and her daughter didn't seem the least bit perturbed. Mama grabbed a chair and slid it over to the foot of the bed, sat down, and lit up a Marlboro Light. I had a strange feeling that the World Health Organization, the Surgeon General, and the American Cancer Society could all walk in at this very instant, see that, and not a single one of them would have the stones to tell her to put it out. Maryse leaned against the chair at her right shoulder.

"You're supposed to be dead. I saw it," I said, eyeing Maryse.

She gave me a look that told me I was absolutely insane.

"You ain't figured it all out yet, have ya?" Mama Duvalier asked.

"Uh, not exactly?"

Mama Duvalier sighed.

"You're pretty, I'll give you that," Maryse chimed in. "You ain't very smart, but you're pretty."

Mama Duvalier took a slow drag off her cigarette.

"Baby," Mama Duvalier said, turning over her shoulder to look at Maryse. "You mind openin' a window?"

Maryse nodded, walked over to the window, and pushed it open. Air, far too cold for the season, rushed in. My skin broke out in goosebumps.

"Feel that?" she asked. "How cold it is?"

"Yeah?"

"Mhm," she said, as if that should explain it all. Obviously, it didn't.

"What?"

"Just the start. You kicked off something big," Mama Duvalier said.

"Such as?"

"I ain't rightly sure, honestly. Big, whatever it is. You can feel it in the air, and I ain't just talking about a cold snap."

I didn't say anything.

"You know that girl you were having a tussle with?" Mama Duvalier continued.

"Lysone?"

"Yeah, but that ain't her name."

"Okay? I'll bite. Who was she?"

"She was a housewife, from Maryland. Been missing for a while. That other one, she played you."

I sat there for a moment, staring between the two of

them, letting the pieces fall where they may in my head. Finally, the light bulb went off. Maryse wasn't dead. Lysone's aura. The stone's reaction to Lysone's death. Kari standing over me when it was all said and done. Those last words before I passed out. Kari had been the one pulling the strings the entire time. She gave Lysone the illusion of power. Killing Maryse, that had been another bit of trickery. I wasn't sure who she was, but Mama Duvalier was a match for most anyone. Kari'd cut me off from an ally that I hadn't even considered. I didn't know to what end. Obviously, to get the stone, but other than that I wasn't sure of much of anything. Maybe it was the pain medication, maybe I wasn't smart enough to see all the pieces, I had no idea. That said, I've been in the game long enough to know, I'd gotten played.

"You killed that poor girl in the circle," Mama Duvalier said, keeping her voice pitched low.

"I finished the spell," I said quietly.

"Mhm."

"So what now?"

"Well first off, a thank you would be nice."

"For?"

"Coming and getting your sorry ass and making sure you didn't die on the side of that damned mountain."

"You brought me here? How did you even…?"

"I kept tabs on you. Wasn't hard. Besides, you got a debt to pay off. You stole from me. Can't have you vanishing on me."

Mama Duvalier stood up, snuffing out her cigarette on the arm of the chair and dropping the butt on the floor. She stood up, put her hands in the back pockets of her jeans, and stared at me.

"We'll talk soon enough. You get yourself better," she said. "You got yourself in a heap of trouble, Jonah. You need to be in fighting shape, given what you've done."

"What have I done?" I asked.

Mama Duvalier stood and turned, walking out, Maryse in tow.

I checked myself out of the hospital the next morning. I found my truck in the parking lot, just outside the emergency room door. I climbed in and sat for a few minutes, happy to be in familiar surroundings. I didn't like the idea of being in debt, this time to someone who made the Carvers look like schoolyard bullies, but I was glad to be alive.

The craving for a drink came a few minutes later, while I was driving through Asheville towards World Coffee. It started out as a nagging urge, but by the time I'd driven a few blocks it was a full-blown roar, tearing through my brain and consuming thoughts at random. It took an almost physical act of will to turn my truck in a direction opposite of Jack of the Wood, but I managed.

Instead, I went home and packed a bag and grabbed another cane. For a minute, I contemplated calling Melly, but in the end decided it was better to just let that dog lie. Instead, I drove to my father's house. It wasn't even eight o'clock in the morning, but he was in the driveway, half buried under the hood of some old muscle car. I dropped my bag on the driveway and walked over to stand beside him, peering down at the massive eight-cylinder engine.

He didn't look up, perfectly content to continue

tinkering with the carburetor, fine tuning with a small screwdriver.

"Start her up," he said, finally, shoving the screwdriver in his back pocket.

I got in the car, and turned the key. The engine kicked over once, then roared to life. He leaned over and adjusted something else, smoothing the idle out to a dull rumble.

"Give it some gas," he said.

I hit the pedal a few times, listening to the massive big block's battle cry.

"Alright, kill it," he said, wiping his hands on a rag.

I got out of the car and walked over to him.

"You look good," he said, eying my face. There was a trace of suspicion there, at the fresh pink scars, but whatever he was thinking, he didn't voice it. Typical for him, really.

"You ready to go," he said.

"Yeah," I said, "Yeah. I am."

He nodded once, and I saw something flash in his eyes. The old man was proud of me.

ACKNOWLEDGMENTS

I don't think anyone writes a book inside of a bubble, though a lot of the time us writer types like to think so. It's a collaborative process, so it's only fair that they get the props they deserve.

So, here goes.

My students, for constantly making me be better than I am. My Padawan, despite her constant reminders that I'm really not much more than a grumpy old man. My brother, Josh, who has this weird way of keeping me in check, whether I need it or not. He really is the best of all of us. Jason, who taught me more about work ethic than probably anyone. To Jonah's first fangirl, since that at least gives me a little reassurance that at least one person will buy this. To the authors that keep inspiring me—Butcher, Hearne, Wendig, King. To my editor Mallory, and the rest of the folks at Diversion, for unprecedented levels of awesome. All the folks I didn't get a chance to mention and all the folks that read the words I put down, you're the awesomest.

PATRICK DONOVAN is the author of the Demon Jack urban fantasy series and the Jonah Heywood urban fantasy series. He currently lives in North Carolina, where he divides his time between teaching, writing, and pursuing a doctoral degree in Special Education. On the off chance he gets a few free minutes, he enjoys fishing, a good cigar, and better coffee.

Printed in the USA
CPSIA information can be obtained
at www.ICGtesting.com
JSHW031711140824
68134JS00038B/3635

9 781635 761788